About the Author

Steven Isserlis was born at a fairly early age. His whole family was musical – his father plays the violin, his mother played the piano, and his two sisters play the violin and viola – so he took up the cello because he didn't want to get left out.

He soon decided that playing the cello was what he wanted to do for the rest of his life (partly because it meant that he wouldn't have to get up too early in the morning to get to work). These days, he travels all over the world, playing concerts to whoever wants to listen (and to a few who don't too) and making recordings – a particular favourite of his is called *Cello World.* He studied in England, Scotland and America; his main teacher was a wonderfully eccentric lady called Jane Cowan who convinced him that he had to become friends with the composers whose music he played. In 1998, he was awarded a CBE, for 'services to music' (though privately, he suspects it was because of his looks); and in 2000, the city of Zwickau (birthplace of the composer Robert Schumann, to whom a chapter of this book is devoted) bestowed the Schumann Prize 2000 upon his curly head. Steven lives in London, with Pauline (who tries to keep him in order), his son Gabriel (who manages to keep him in disorder), lots of cellos and a piano. He has quite a few hobbies, but what he likes best (apart from listening to music and reading books, perhaps) is to eat lots of food.

First published in 2001
by Faber and Faber Limited
Bloomsbury House, 74-77 Great Russell Street, London, WC1B 3DA

Designed by Mackerel
Printed in the UK by CPI Group (UK) Ltd, Croydon, CR0 4YY

A CIP record for this book
is available from the British Library

ISBN 978-0-571-20616-2
ISBN 0-571-20616-6

16

Why Beethoven Threw the Stew

Steven Isserlis
Illustrations by Adam Stower

faber and faber

To Gabriel (as always), and to my lovely nieces Isabel and Natasha; but also to Stepan Chilingirian, Yuval Shallon, Benjamin Doane and all my other young friends who have convinced me that children are the BEST THING.

A Note for Parents

Each chapter is in three parts: a portrait of the composer, which children can read (or have read to them); a brief description of the music, with a guide to some pieces that the children may particularly enjoy; and a short biography of each composer, with more stories relating to their lives, which may be dipped into, or read in one go.

Contents

Introduction

Music is a sort of magic. Who invented it? Nobody knows. Where does it come from? Nobody knows. Who composes it? Nobody kn- no, hang on; we DO know that. Composers compose it. They write down a series of dots and lines on a page; then performers come along with their instruments and voices, look at the dots and lines on the page, and make sounds from them. It's all very mysterious. Or is it? After all, these words you're reading are just another series of dots and lines; you know what they mean, so you can look at them and make sounds (and sense) from them. So maybe music is really just another language, with its own meaning; but there IS something more magical about music than about any other language. The range of sounds is far, far huger than that of any spoken language; and because they aren't tied to any specific meaning, the sounds can express much more. There's no musical sound meaning 'sausage' or 'dirty laundry', for instance; but on the other hand, a musical sentence, or phrase, can sound happy, sad, thoughtful, nostalgic and eager – all at the same time! Words would get exhausted if they tried to express as many meanings as that. Perhaps one day we'll arrive at a distant planet, millions of light-years away, and discover a race of beings who speak only in music; but they'd have to be a lot more sophisticated than we are.

I've been lucky, in musical terms. I was brought up in a house full of the sounds of it. My father played the violin, my mother the piano (and clarinet for a bit, until we stuffed a tissue up it when she wasn't looking, so that she would decide that it was broken, and stop practising at all hours – mean of us, I know, but it worked), my elder sister the viola and piano and my middle sister the violin and piano. We also had a dog called Dandy (long since departed for the great lamp-post in the sky, unfortunately) who, when we played a certain piece by Mozart on the piano, would get up on his armchair, prop his short legs on the side of it, and howl his little heart out. If we went wrong, and he didn't recognise it any more, he'd give us a foul look, snort disgustedly and go off to sleep. So, thanks to my family, I always knew the names in this book – Bach, Mozart, Beethoven and so on; but I didn't know that much about them. It was only when I started learning the cello with my main teacher, a lady called Jane Cowan, that I really started to get to know them as people; she brought them alive! She would quote bits of their letters, tell stories about them, laugh at the musical jokes they'd put into their pieces; in fact, she encouraged me to make friends with them. Great friends they turned out to be, too. Of course, there were limits: for instance, I couldn't really call up Mozart when I was feeling miserable; people who have been dead since 1791 are extremely hard to reach by phone. But I could at least read about his life, and listen to his music; and that kept me endlessly fascinated then – and keeps me endlessly fascinated now.

You probably know the feeling, when you have two friends who don't know each other, and you're sure they'd like each other: you can't wait to introduce them – and then you really hope they'll hit it off. Well, that was really my reason for writing this book. I was lucky enough to 'meet' all these composers when I was a child – brilliant, sometimes extremely difficult, sometimes very funny, always wonderfully alive people. And I wanted you to meet them too, so that you could have these friends-for-life who continue to talk to us today, long dead though they all are, through their music. I hope you get along!

So finally – why DID Beethoven throw the stew? Well, to be completely honest, he didn't – it was just a plate of veal with lots of gravy; but somehow 'Why Beethoven Threw the Veal with Lots of Gravy' just didn't have a *ring* to it. Apart from that, though, I've tried to be as accurate as possible; one doesn't need to invent things about these composers' lives – they were more amazing in themselves than anything I could invent. So read on, and you'll find out, not just why Beethoven spilled the gravy, but also why Bach walked for 400 kilometres (250 miles to us oldies), why Mozart's hairdresser got stuck, why Stravinsky got arrested with one famous painter and missed his lunch appointment with another – and so on. Have fun!

Steven Isserlis

Johann Sebastian Bach

1685-1750

I do hope that it will never happen; but if ever I were to be strolling along a beach and were to come across an interesting-looking bottle with an old cork in it, and were to remove the cork; and if a huge green genie were to swarm out of the bottle and, instead of thanking me for freeing him from the bottle and saving him from cramp, were to boom out, "I grant you a choice: for the rest of your life, you may listen to the music of just one composer. Now – choose!" – what would I say?

Well, I think that I would first point out – very politely (maybe I'm old-fashioned, but I do believe in being thoroughly polite to fierce green monsters who are hovering menacingly over my head) – that most genies freed from bottles would, as a rule, offer me three nice wishes, not one choice that would actually stop me listening to the music of hundreds of composers that I love. Perhaps at this point the genie would blush, bite his green lip, and mutter, "Whoops! so sorry, master – my mistake; a slip of the tongue. Please wish away

all you like, three times over – no, four times over
– one extra as an apology for my silliness."
On the other hand, perhaps he
wouldn't; perhaps he would boom
out, "One composer, I said – and
that's what I meant. Now stop
arguing, or I'll stuff *you* into the
bottle!" At which point I would
(rather hurriedly) answer, "All
right, O Not-Very-Gentle Genie: if I
must choose just the one composer, and
stick with him for life, it would have to be –
Johann Sebastian Bach."

Now, supposing that the genie were to vanish at
this point (at which I'd heave a huge sigh of relief – a thoroughly
charmless object, in my humble opinion) and *you* were to take his
place; and instead of floating over my head, you were to plant
yourself squarely in front of me, fold your arms defiantly, and say,
"Oh yeah? So what was so great about this Johann Sebastian Bach?
And what was he like?" – what would I say to that?

Well, I'd probably shuffle a bit, look at my shoes, and then reply
something like this, "What was so great about him was his music –
it was – it is – total genius! Every note that he ever wrote sounds
completely right! And he wrote some of the saddest music there is,
some of the happiest music, some of the most beautiful, the most
exciting..." "Yes," you might interrupt (a touch rude, but let it pass,
let it pass – I was getting a bit boring, I know) "but what was he *like*?"
"Ah," I'd say carefully, "I'm glad you asked me that; well, actually, I'm
not *that* glad that you asked me that. In fact, to tell you the truth,
I'm not *at all* glad that you asked me that; because the fact is that
there you have me on toast – because we really don't know *what* he
was like!" It's true: all we really know about him is that he was a very
successful musician who had a series of jobs playing the organ in
churches, giving concerts, providing music for princes, dukes and

local bigwigs, teaching young musicians and so on – just like lots of other professional musicians in Germany at the time. We don't even know whether he realised that he was a genius! (My guess is that he did, though – even though he might not have admitted it.)

At least we know roughly what he looked like; one portrait of him, painted when he was about sixty, has survived from his time. Actually, he looks rather fierce – not at all like his wise, kind music. He's frowning out of the picture at us – maybe he's telling us to go and listen to his music, if we want to know what he's like! He's wearing an enormous, white, curly wig. (I bet he was bald underneath that wig. Bald Bach.) And he's – er – plump – well-filled – a healthy size. Oh, all right – he's a bit fat – if you insist. He certainly liked his food and drink; if friends wanted to get into his good books, they'd send him either a good joint of meat, or a good bottle of brandy or wine. In fact, for some of his early jobs, part of his yearly salary would be paid in beer! And when he shut himself away in his private studio to compose, he'd often take a bottle of brandy with him. I wonder how he kept his head clear enough to compose? Well, obviously he had no problem.

Another thing that Bach liked, probably even more than his food and drink, was his family. He came from one of the most musical families of all time. His great-great-grandfather Veit (pronounced 'Fight') Bach (pronounced, by the way, halfway between a sheep's 'baa' and a dog's 'bark' – with the 'ch' sounding as if you were trying to clear your throat) was a baker, who couldn't bear to be without his musical instrument, a very old sort of guitar called the cittern (pronounced 'sittern'). He used to take it into his bakery with him and play away to his heart's content while the corn was being ground to make bread. His two sons caught the 'music bug' and passed it on to their children, who passed it on to theirs – and so on. Over the next fifty years or so, more than seventy-five Bachs became professional musicians – more than fifty of them called Johann (and not one of them called Marmaduke, strangely enough); in the area where most of them lived, the word Bach actually came to *mean* musician!

When our Bach – Johann (pronounced 'Yohann' – right; that's the end of the pronunciation lesson) Sebastian – was growing up, the whole family used to get together once a year for enormous parties. Being devout Christians, they'd start off by singing hymns. (It's not surprising that one of Bach's favourite passages in the Bible is one that describes 288 members of the same tribe playing religious music together.) When the serious stuff was over, though, they'd start to sing funny songs, and would compose accompaniments to them as they went along, and change the words and the notes to make each other laugh, and generally have a grand old time. They didn't even need computer games to keep them amused! Ahem.

Our Bach didn't do too badly in his contribution to the family – he had twenty children! Sadly, ten of them died while still very young – very common in those days; but even ten children isn't bad going, really. Three and a half of his sons became famous composers too. (Well – three of them were famous, one half-famous).

Bach had two wives (not at the same time, I hasten to add). The first, Maria Barbara, was his first cousin (I told you he liked his family!) He was blissfully happy with her, and they had seven children together; but one day he got back from a long trip (it took much longer to get anywhere then because one had to travel everywhere by horse-and-carriage – or on foot) and found that his wife was dead! He'd left her quite healthy, and came back to find that she was already buried. No telephones then, so no way of warning him – what a shock.

The next year, though, he got married again, this time to a non-relative, a singer called Anna Magdalena. He must have been wildly excited about the marriage: he spent a fifth of his annual salary just on the wine for the wedding party! (Ask a grown-up to calculate what a fifth of their salary would come to; then ask them if they'd be willing to pay that just for the wine for one party. I can imagine their answer...) Anna Magdalena seems to have been a wonderful person, and they must have been a great team, but a frantic one. For her part, as well as bearing thirteen children – can you imagine it? – she had to look after the four who had survived from Bach's first marriage, and also the various other relatives who came to live in the house. She sang at many of Bach's concerts; she studied the harpsichord (an older brother of the piano) and probably the organ with him; and she copied out Bach's new pieces. (I wonder if she ever washed his wig?) She also managed to find time – how? – for gardening; she loved flowers and birds. There were often visitors, too; the Bachs used to give dinner parties. Probably the guests were entertained by the whole Bach family, singing and playing music together. Their house must have been a noisy, but fun, place to be.

Bach can't have spent all that much time there with his wife and children, though – he was busy! For a start, of course, he was constantly composing; today it would take a normal person years just to copy out all his music, even working twenty-four hours a day. (And that's not counting the huge number of pieces that, annoyingly, have been lost since Bach wrote them.) He was also the greatest organist and harpsichordist of his time; people would go into raptures about the pieces he made up on the spot – so beautiful, so brilliant, so complicated! But when can he have practised? Every musician, even a genius, has to practise to keep up his or her playing. Bach had to teach his pupils for hours each day, rehearse the choir and orchestra for weekly church services and for weekly concerts, conduct, play the violin and viola, tune his own keyboard instruments, examine lots of newly built organs (nobody knew as much about them, and how they worked, as him), invent new instruments for his own pieces if he wanted new sounds – and to write incredibly long and boring letters to his employers complaining about all sorts of things – mostly related to money. Hmm... maybe that last bit isn't that impressive. But the rest certainly is: how on earth did he manage to fit it all in? Maybe he only slept five minutes a night – and all his days were forty-eight hours long!

Now – what's this? I hear a small, but insistent voice, in my ear – where's it coming from? Ah – it's *you*! Still standing there, with your arms folded. (Aren't they sore by now?) "So," you say firmly, "now we know what he *did* – but what was he LIKE?"

All right – I'll tell you (very briefly) what I think he must have been like as a person. We know that he was happily married, twice over, that he had lots of friends, and that he was *mostly* very friendly to other musicians; but also that he could be extremely *un*friendly to people he didn't like. He was always quarrelling with his employers, whether they were officials at a royal court, or members of town councils. Almost the only letters of his that survive are complaining letters addressed to 'your magnificences, most noble, most learned and most honourable sirs and patrons!' – but if you read the letters, you realise that Bach would much rather have addressed them as 'your twitships, most stupid, most annoying and most cabbage-headed idiots and morons!' He couldn't stand most of them; and they couldn't stand him. He was always wanting more money out of them – not necessarily for himself (although he wouldn't have minded that!); but primarily so that he could hire more, and better, musicians to perform his music. He wanted perfection; and all his employers wanted was a quiet, normal life. Although Bach was generally described as 'amiable', he cared so much about music that he could all too easily lose his temper over it. When he was young, he got into a sword-fight with a student whose bassoon-playing Bach didn't like; and later in life, he got so furious with a musician for playing wrong notes that he snatched the wig off his own head, and hurled it at him! He could forget his manners in formal situations, too. Once Bach went to a party, and arrived as a harpsichordist was playing. Seeing the great Bach, the harpsichordist immediately stopped, right in the middle of a phrase. Bach couldn't bear the music being broken off so abruptly; ignoring his host's outstretched hand and polite greeting, Bach rushed past him to the harpsichord and finished off the phrase! So maybe that's why he looks cross in the portrait: he was probably so wrapped up in music, so full of it at all times, that nothing else entered his mind. Sitting for a portrait might well have felt to him like a waste of time – perhaps the artist was talking to Bach as he painted, distracting him from the music in his head ? I can imagine that if someone was trying to talk to him about a thoroughly fascinating topic, such as the weather that day, or the weather the next day, or possibly the weather the previous day, Bach might be looking at them; but his mind would be preoccupied with his next piece, or perhaps with who would perform his last piece the most beautifully. So he probably wasn't an easy man to get to know, or to get along with.

I would guess that the best, perhaps the only, way to become his friend would be to talk about music – and to play it – with him. To be conducted by him in his church must have been amazing. He'd be sitting at the organ, playing incredibly complicated passages with both hands, and with his feet (on the organ pedals); then he'd be directing the choir and orchestra with his head, hearing everything, seeing everything, singing out the right notes if anyone went wrong, showing one group where to come in with one of his fingers, another group with another finger, and showing the whole expression of the piece with his face, so that everybody became as passionately involved as him. That's where he was surely at his happiest, and most awe-inspiring; so maybe that's where we'll leave him – bye-bye, Father Bach!

The Music

The music of most composers, even the greatest, varies in quality. Next to the masterpieces, there are usually works for which one has to apologise a bit: "Oh, he was just experimenting when he wrote that," or "That one was written in a hurry." But in Bach's case, I have never heard a piece that didn't seem – to me, at least – perfect, every note inspired; and the strange thing is that he was always experimenting, and he was always in a hurry! (Possibly a couple of his very first works aren't completely earth-shattering; but he soon outgrew such flashes of normal human weakness.) He used to compose his pieces in his head, and then write them down; he hardly ever used pencil when he wrote them out – he would go straight into ink. (And on the rare occasions when he made a mistake, he would have to scratch out the wrong note

with a knife.) He did revise some works, improving and refining them; but he always ended up with something sublime, and seemingly effortlessly written. Bach's music can be deeply sad; one of his very greatest works is the 'St. Matthew Passion', based on the Gospel of St. Matthew in the New Testament from the Bible, telling the story of the crucifixion of Jesus Christ. It lasts almost three hours, and seems to explore every possible shade of grief. But his music can also be wonderfully happy, full of fizzy, dancing rhythms and smiley tunes – the 'Brandenburg Concertos', for instance. This was a set of six orchestral pieces that he wrote featuring all sorts of different solo instruments, including the trumpet and recorder – together! A strange combination – one of the loudest instruments playing with one of the softest – but in Bach's hands, it works. His music can be comforting and peaceful, too; his Chorale Preludes for the organ contain some of the most serene, radiant music ever written. Whether he's writing tragic or joyous music, though, it's never as if Bach is telling us about his own sadness or happiness; it's more as if a wise father is watching his children from above, as they go about their sad or happy lives. For Bach, who was deeply religious, music and religion were almost the same thing; making music was a way of worshipping God. Everything he wrote was, as he put it, dedicated to the 'glory of God and the recreation of the soul'. But if that sounds rather forbidding – it isn't! His music is never pompous; it pulses with energy, humour, compassion and beauty. And above all it makes you feel glad to be alive!

What to listen to

Well, you can't go wrong with Bach; as I said, there's no such thing as a bad piece by him. Maybe you should start with fun music, such as the 'Brandenburg Concertos' – perhaps No. 3; if you feel like dancing to it, go ahead! Then you could try the 'Goldberg Variations' for harpsichord (often played on the piano these days).

This set of thirty variations on a beautiful theme was apparently written by Bach as a gift for a nobleman, a Count, who had trouble sleeping. When he was awake in the middle of the night, he'd wake up a very young (and probably very tired) harpsichordist called Goldberg whom he employed, and make him play some of the variations. The 'Goldberg Variations' have a huge range of moods and colours; if you prefer, you can be like the sleepless Count, and listen to just one or two of them at a time. And so on – there are so many masterpieces that you can't really go wrong – just look for the name 'J.S. Bach' on the packet! If I had to name just one work, though, I think I'd choose the 'St. Matthew Passion'. Since it's so long, I'd suggest that you listen to it in little bits to start with; get to know it gradually from a recording. Eventually, when you feel ready to sit and take the whole thing in, go to a performance; it can be an overwhelming experience. And the more you hear it, the more you'll get out of it.

Facts of Life

Bach's father, Johann Ambrosius, was – surprise surprise – a musician. He was director of music at the little town of Eisenach, where Bach was born on March 21st, 1685. J. A. Bach had had a big success when he'd first taken up the post fourteen years earlier, when he'd arranged a concert featuring organ, violins, voices, trumpets and military drums – what a racket! So it's safe to assume that our Bach must have grown up in a fairly noisy environment. Unfortunately, his mother, Maria Elisabeth, died when Bach was only nine. His father remarried less than seven months later; in true Bach style, he kept it in the family, marrying the widow of a cousin of his. Perhaps this second marriage was a bit much for him to cope with, though; within four months, Johann Ambrosius was dead himself. His widow wrote sadly to the town council of Eisenach asking for support, saying that she'd need it because there was no musical talent left in the Bach family. Not EXACTLY accurate...

Two peas in a pod...

Johann Ambrosius had a twin called Johann Christoph. It was said that the brothers did everything exactly the same – played music the same way, got ill at the same time, talked and thought exactly alike. In fact, people even said that they looked so similar that their wives couldn't tell them apart! I find that very hard to believe; surely no wife would ever make the mistake of scolding her brother-in-law for staying out too late at the pub...

Poor Johann Sebastian, not yet ten years old, was now an orphan. His eldest brother, Johann Christoph (yes, I know that that was his uncle's name too – don't blame me! It's not my fault) was an organist living nearby, and little Bach and another brother, Jacob, were packed off to live with him. Can you imagine being brought up by an elder brother? Strange. Mind you, Johann Christoph was fourteen years older, so maybe he seemed more like a young father.

Midnight visit...

*Johann Christoph was responsible for Bach's education – including, of course, his musical education. Bach progressed **too** well on the harpsichord for his brother's liking, soon getting bored with the student pieces he was supposed to learn, and begging his brother to let him look at a book of grown-up pieces that Johann Christoph owned. When this request was refused, Johann Sebastian took to getting up in the middle of the night, stealing the book out of a cupboard and copying it out by moonlight. (He* *wasn't allowed a candle at night. I wonder what happened when he needed to go to the loo?) It took him six months to finish copying it – but, as soon as he had, his brother found out about it and locked away both copies for good. Spoilsport.*

Bach was eventually sent to school, where he did brilliantly. He managed to pay some of the expenses of his education himself, partly by coaching richer boys in Latin, and partly by singing in the choir – his first experience as a professional musician.

A problem comes up (or down)...

Bach had a fine high singing voice as boy; but one day he opened his mouth to say something – and a two-part voice came out! There was his old high voice, plus a new low one. For the next eight days, every time he spoke or sang, the same strange double-noise would come out. After that, the low voice won, and Bach had lost his lovely boy's voice – and with it, his place in the choir.

As Bach grew up, he became more and more fascinated by music, and wanted to learn more and more about it. There were no recordings in those days, of course, so if he wanted to hear a famous organist or harpsichordist, he had to find out where they would be playing, and somehow get there. When he was young, he couldn't often afford to go by coach; once he had to travel 400 kilometres (250 miles) – as far as he ever travelled in his whole life on foot to hear a famous organist – phew! Can you imagine doing that? I hope the organist was worth it!

A lucky break...

Coming back from one of his listening trips, Bach had run out of money – and he wasn't even half way home. He passed an inn, and smelled food cooking – torture! Suddenly, he heard a window opening, and saw a couple of herring heads being thrown out. That may sound a bit revolting to us, but to the starving Bach they looked delicious, and he grabbed them, opened them up – and found a gold coin inside each one! Was this just extraordinary luck – or had some anonymous person seen him, and taken pity on him? We'll never know.

From the age of eighteen, Bach supported himself with a series of jobs at small towns not far from his birthplace. These were very useful for him, not just because of the income, but also because they gave him the chance to develop musically – to try things out, to compose different kinds of music for different occasions, and to perform with other musicians. He must have been frustrated at times, though; the boring old Town Councils were always telling him off, or just ignoring him. At one place, he was reprimanded for taking too much time off without leave (he'd gone to listen to another organist); then he was told off for playing for too long at church services; then he was told off for not playing long enough at church services; and then he was told off for inviting a lady into the choir-loft, and 'making music' with her there! Ahem. At the next place, three of the councillors, asked to sign a letter offering Bach the job, declared that they were much too upset about a recent fire in the town to think about mere music – and besides, they didn't have any pens or ink with them! And at the next town, when Bach told his bosses that he wanted to leave to take a better post, he got thrown into jail for almost a month. Of course, being Bach, he spent the month composing; but, since he wasn't allowed pen or paper, it had to be all done in his head, and written down when he finally got home – what an incredible memory he must have had.

By the time he was in his early thirties...

...Bach had become famous as a brilliant organist and harpsichordist. Rather like pop or jazz musicians today, performers then were expected to play their own compositions, either making them up as they went along or writing them out for themselves and others to play. His reputation had spread as far as the major city of Dresden, where a French organist and harpsichordist called Marchand was having a great success. Someone decided that there should be a musical competition between Bach and Marchand, and Bach was summoned to Dresden. He got there, and waited with several knowledgeable types for Marchand to arrive – but he never showed up. It turned out that when Marchand realised that he was really going to have to play against the famous Bach, he'd panicked, ordered a special coach, and had himself driven back to France as fast as the horses' eight legs could carry him!

For the last twenty-seven years of his life, Bach lived and worked in the city of Leipzig. Today, the city is visited every year by thousands of 'Bach tourists', eager to see the places where their hero performed some of his greatest works for the first time. They can see the churches where congregations of around two thousand people would have been stunned by the music coming out of the choir-loft; at one stage, Bach was producing a new cantata (a big piece for singers and orchestra) every week – it would have taken most composers months! Unfortunately, they can't see the school where he lived and taught or the coffee-house where he used to give his famous weekly concerts with his musicians – the buildings are long gone. (Just the door to the school has been preserved and can be seen in a local museum.) In fact, even those buildings that remain have changed hugely since Bach was in them; but maybe his spirit is still there, hovering around wearing a ghostly wig?

Of course...

...Bach didn't get on very well with the authorities in Leipzig (surprise, surprise). He was always being annoyed by something or other – either for good musical reasons, or for slightly less good reasons, almost always related to money. In one letter, for instance, he is very cross because a Leipziger has got married outside the city – according to Bach, just to avoid having to pay for the wedding-music; in another letter, he complains that there has been too healthy a wind blowing in the town that year, and so he isn't getting his extra fees for funerals! Hmm...

Towards the end of his life, Bach went to Berlin to visit one of his sons, who was then a musician at the court of the famous king

Frederick the Great. The King was informed that Bach had arrived. "Gentlemen!" he announced excitedly to his courtiers, "Old Bach is here!" Bach was immediately dragged into the room – rather embarrassed, because he was still dressed in his travelling clothes – and ordered to perform on the King's pianos. (The piano was just being developed then, and the King was very keen on this newfangled instrument – keener than Bach was, in fact.) Bach played – brilliantly, of course; and while everybody was gasping and swooning away, Bach topped it all by inviting the King to compose a tune, around which Bach would invent a whole piece. (Bach could hear any tune and know immediately what could be done with it, by himself or anybody else. If he was listening to a new piece by another composer, he would turn to his neighbour after just a few moments, and whisper to him exactly what was going to happen as the piece went on. When he was proved right – as he always was – he would nudge his neighbour in an 'I-told-you-so' sort of way; poor neighbour!) Not only did Bach immediately play a whole piece based on the King's theme: when he got back to Leipzig, he composed a huge work, containing several different pieces, all based on the King's theme, and published it under the polite title 'The Musical Offering'. Frederick the Great should have been thrilled! Maybe he was – but he had a strange way of showing it; he immediately gave the music away to his sister, who was actually a student of Bach's. Rather an odd way to treat a precious gift, I'd say.

The whispering room...

While Bach was in Berlin, his son took him to the new Opera House. One feature of the building was a huge dining room: the moment Bach entered it, he pointed out something that nobody, not even the architects who had built it, had noticed. He said that if someone went to one corner of the vast room and whispered something very quietly, another person standing in the opposite corner of the room, facing the wall, would hear it all quite distinctly – while no-one in the middle of the room would hear a thing. Bach was quite right – needless to say; he always was!

As he grew very old (for those days, when people tended to die much younger) Bach's general health remained good, and his mind was as active as ever; but he started to go blind. The delightful Leipzig Town Council, realising that they might finally get rid of the man who was always causing them trouble, promptly brought in a rather mediocre musician to do an entrance examination for the post of successor of Bach, who had not even died yet! Bach was furious: there he was, struggling to get better, still full of musical projects – and here was the Town Council, already plotting and planning to replace him! He did get better for a bit – maybe just to annoy them; but it didn't last, and eventually Bach had to have an operation on his eyes. It was performed by an Englishman, Dr. Taylor, who wrote later that he had treated 'a vast variety of singular animals, such as dromedaries, camels, etc., and ... a celebrated master of music'. A peculiar list! Anyway, no matter how successful he'd been with his camels and dromedaries, he failed with Bach; and Bach died on July 28th, 1750, aged sixty-five. At the time of his death, he was famous within his own part of Germany, but not really known anywhere else. It was only gradually, over the next fifty years or so, people started to look carefully at the music he had left behind, and began to realise that he was one of the greatest geniuses who had ever lived.

But before he died...

*One of Bach's last major works was called 'The Art of Fugue'. A fugue (pronounced 'fewg' – whoops; I said I'd finished with the pronunciation lesson – sorry!) is a piece of music in which all that happens, really, is that a fairly short theme, or series of notes, is used over and over again in all sorts of different ways. It is supposed to be the most difficult sort of piece for a composer to write well and interestingly. No new, completely different themes allowed – just the one, which often isn't much of a tune anyway; it must be rather like having to write a whole play in which all the characters do is discuss one idea. But 'The Art of Fugue' is amazing. It has eighteen different movements, all based on the same little theme. Some of the movements can be played backwards or upside-down! Unfortunately, the version we have is incomplete: it probably **was** finished, but the manuscript which survives breaks off in the middle of the last fugue; maybe his health failed as he was copying it out, and he had to give up. The complete version is probably lost for ever. (Various people have tried to finish this last fugue, with varying success; but when it's played in concerts, musicians usually break off in mid-phrase – as the manuscript does.) As Bach lay dying, according to legend, he composed a new version of an organ piece he'd written earlier, and dictated it to a friend or pupil, who wrote it out at Bach's bedside. It is based on an old hymn, of which the first line reads: 'Before Your Throne I Now Appear'; it is clear that, his head full as ever of music (and religion), Bach was ready to die peacefully.*

Of Bach's ten children who survived infancy, one, a son who had got into all sorts of scrapes and caused his father great sorrow, was already dead; three were unmarried daughters, who kept Anna Magdalena company in Leipzig until she died, ten years after Bach. Another daughter was married to one of Bach's favourite pupils, and also looked after another son of Bach's, who needed constant care; and the other four sons all became composers. Since their names are a bit long-winded, it's probably easier to refer to them by their initials: the eldest, W. F. Bach, was perhaps the most talented, but made rather an unfortunate mess of his life; C. P. E. Bach was much more responsible, married a rich lady – always useful! – and became very famous, his works still being performed very often today. J. C. Bach moved to London, made lots of money with his music, and was a bit of a rogue; and J. C. F. Bach, although the least interesting composer of the four, was known to be an exceedingly kind, amiable person.

After he died...

...Bach left most of his manuscripts of his works to his sons; they must have appreciated the treasure they'd inherited, but nevertheless, much of Bach's music has been lost. W. F. Bach sold his share when he ran out of money – luckily most of it, but not all, to C. P. E. Bach; J. C. F. Bach's share vanished too, somehow – maybe he was so amiable that he gave it all away! C.P. E. Bach was the only one who really took care of his pile of manuscripts, buying more of them whenever he could, and incidentally making quite a lot of money out of having them published;

while J. C. Bach, who inherited lots of instruments from his father, and maybe therefore not so much music, probably didn't appreciate his father's genius at all. He used to refer to Bach as 'the Old Wig'; the Old Wig, indeed – the cheek of it! Oh well – he was the youngest and most fashion-conscious of all the brothers – perhaps he never really grew up; and perhaps his father wouldn't have loved him any the less for it...

Wolfgang Amadeus Mozart

1756-1791

Have you ever seen a cheetah or a jaguar (the animal, not the car) running? They're amazing; they run so fast, so gracefully – and so easily. What would they think if they saw a human being trying to run next to them? I'd imagine that if they weren't too distracted by the thought of how nice this person would taste with an antelope salad, they'd probably wonder why the human was so slow and clumsy, and why everything looked so awkward.

In musical terms, Mozart (pronounced 'Moats - art') was a bit like a cheetah or jaguar. Music just wasn't difficult for him! He learnt to understand music as he learnt to understand speech; for him, it was just another language. Music was part of him, and he needed it like an animal needs food. As a child, Mozart – whose first name was Wolfgang, pronounced 'Volfgang' – would pounce on any new piece he was given. From the age of four, he started to play little pieces on the piano or harpsichord, and could learn them perfectly in half-an-hour. He started to compose at the age of five; and shortly after that, he became a brilliant organist, an excellent violinist and an able singer. (He would sing, in his rather wavery, thin little voice, duets with his father Leopold – and get very cross when Leopold made any mistakes.) At the age of twelve, he composed his first opera, and was by then already a fine conductor. It must have looked funny when this little boy sternly conducted an orchestra of professionals three or four times his age. But he brought it off – because everybody realised that he was a total miracle.

He was utterly adorable, too; it was impossible not to love him for his sweet disposition and lively, fun-loving character. He looked beautiful, as well. His face was distinguished by neat, regular features, with a winningly gentle expression; and to complete the wonderful impression he made on everybody, he would dress up for special occasions in the finest clothes (miniature ones, of course) with a splendiferous curly wig to match. But for all his sophisticated charm, Mozart was a bit like an animal in all sorts of ways: he was as bright as a hamster's eyes, as playful as a kitten and as affectionate as a puppy. He was always needing to be reassured that the people around him loved him (they all did); and even as a little youngster, he was constantly falling in love with beautiful ladies. He once developed a crush on Marie Antoinette (later to be Queen of France, and later still to lose, or at least mislay, her head – extremely careless of her) and informed her, much to her amusement, that he was going to marry her. When he grew a bit older, this little animal developed a sense of humour that was extremely animal-like, as well. He could be really funny; but he could also be absolutely disgusting. He was obsessed with happenings in the bathroom, and related smells – (as were his parents, for that matter;) he would write – well, enough. You can imagine the rest...

All right – enough imagining! To get back to the innocent child: Mozart was obviously such a genius that Papa Leopold (a violinist, composer and music teacher) decided that what the world really needed was to hear Wolfgang, along with his pianist/harpsichordist sister Maria Anna (known as 'Nannerl'), play. So, waving a not-very-fond farewell to their native Salzburg, where the Mozart family felt trapped – it was a small town, with extremely limited opportunities for young miracles – they embarked upon a huge series of tours to the great cities of Europe. (Great for us, by the way, because Leopold started to write long letters to his friends back in Salzburg, boasting of Wolfgang and Nannerl's triumphs; these letters, and later ones between the family, give us a huge amount of information about Mozart's life – all of which is today studied, analysed, dissected, held upside-down and read back-to-front, etc., by 'Mozart scholars' the world over.) The children gave concerts everywhere – usually starting with Nannerl playing difficult pieces brilliantly, and then being upstaged (poor Nannerl) by her little brother. He would not only play equally difficult works – even if he'd never seen them before – and duets on one keyboard with his sister (quite a novelty for those times), but would make up on the spot huge pieces based on tunes suggested to him by his audience. People didn't believe that he was really doing it all without any preparation; they kept trying to catch him out – they'd spread a cloth over the keyboard (a strange thing to do, but they did it anyway), smile knowingly at each other, and wait for little Wolfgang to make a fool of himself. It didn't work – he played just as amazingly as before. Then someone would offer to sing a complicated song, but apologise for having left the music at home – probably winking at the rest of the audience the while. No problem – Wolfgang would listen to the song once, and then make up any number of wonderful accompaniments, probably much better than the original composer's version. Of course, audiences just worshipped him – all the more so because if he felt he'd been over-praised, he'd get really upset, and burst into tears.

This was all great, in some ways; but there were drawbacks. For a start, Mozart was being treated a bit like a performing animal – which was wrong, even if he was *like* an animal. Although he was a musical phenomenon, he was still a normal child in other ways – and he wasn't having a normal childhood. His health suffered from all the travelling. The journeys, in horse-drawn carriages, took ages, and were usually really uncomfortable; sometimes Mozart had to lift himself up by the hands for hours on end, just to stop his rear end being bruised by all the bumping! All his musical work was a strain, too, much though he enjoyed it; he would be up at all hours composing or performing. His health problems in later years probably stemmed from this unnatural lifestyle. And worst of all – in Leopold's eyes, anyway – was that, despite all the acclaim and adoration, the Mozarts weren't earning all that much money. So in many ways, life was hard; and, wonderful though it was to be born a genius, perhaps Mozart's life would have been easier if he'd been born normal. But ours wouldn't be, because we wouldn't have his music...

Well, that was Mozart the child; now you'd better fasten your seat-belt pretty tightly, because we're going to do a bit of time-travelling. All buckled up? Good – now let's LEAP forward several years... And who is this elegant fellow we see before us? It's Mozart – what a coincidence! He's now in Vienna, the great capital of Austria. It took him years – until he was twenty-five, in fact – to free himself from Salzburg, with all its small-minded gossip. Actually, he only exchanged it, really, for the small-minded gossip of Vienna – but at least there were many more people to gossip with in Vienna, and they gossiped in a much wittier, more sophisticated way. Making a career in Vienna was quite a struggle, but he still preferred it to Salzburg. In Salzburg, he'd been in the service of the Archbishop, who treated him like a servant, and paid him a pittance; Mozart longed to leave, but couldn't quite do it. Then, when Mozart had already become quite famous internationally as an opera composer, and had just had a big success in Munich, the Archbishop went on an official trip to Vienna, and summoned Mozart to go with him as a member of his household. Mozart, who didn't want to go anyway, was forced to take his meals with the valets and cooks, and was prevented from giving concerts for other important people (who would have paid him handsomely). Eventually, Mozart complained, told the Archbishop just what he thought of him, received his low opinions back with interest from the Archbishop (in language quite unbecoming for an official of the Church) and was booted out of his job – literally – by the Archbishop's right-hand man, who gave Mozart a huge kick on the bum! Hmm... a rather unglamorous way to have a career launched – but it did do the trick. Freed of his Salzburg shackles, Mozart didn't take too long to become very famous, giving masses of concerts, in which he played his own piano music with joyous brilliance and conducted his stunning new orchestral works; he also wrote more operas and chamber-music, and was acknowledged by many as the finest musician alive. (Even Joseph Haydn – pronounced Hide-un – the other greatest composer of the time, told Leopold when he met him that 'your son is the greatest composer known to me either in person or by name'; quite a compliment from another genius.)

Now, as an adult in his late twenties, the Mozart that we see is a very different being from the adorable child he'd been in earlier years. He's still small – though not *that* small – but with a rather large head, and skin pockmarked by the smallpox he'd had as an eleven-year-old. He has dispensed with the wig, and wears his own hair, powdered and carefully shaped – and mighty proud of it he is, too. (No matter how busy Mozart's schedule was, he'd always start the day, usually at six in the morning – yuk – by having his hair neatly patterned by the hairdresser. Sometimes he'd forget that he was having it done, because a new musical idea occurred to him; he'd get up and note down the idea, dragging the hapless hairdresser, still holding on to Mozart's pigtails, after him.) We should also meet his wife, Constanze: at the age of twenty-six, Mozart had married the twenty-year-old singer Constanze Weber (pronounced 'Vayber'). Earlier, Mozart had fallen in love with Constanze's older sister Aloysia – much to the dismay of Leopold, who was thoroughly suspicious of the whole Weber family. Several years after Aloysia had rejected him and broken his heart, Mozart, his heart mysteriously mended, settled for her younger sister – at which point Leopold was practically foaming at the mouth. Mozart sang Constanze's praises to his father, assuring him that she wasn't very pretty, but had a heart of gold and would help him live economically. (Not exactly the most romantic of descriptions, but he knew what would impress his eternally suspicious father). It was no good, though; neither Leopold or Nannerl ever seem to have warmed to Constanze. There was nothing they could do about the marriage, however – and their suspicions just seem to have irritated Mozart, who thereafter grew less close to his father and sister. Wolfgang and Constanze seem to have been very happy together – apart from the odd moment when Mozart would catch Constanze flirting with other men, which would annoy him greatly; but perhaps she was just making sure that he appreciated her...

In some ways, Leopold was right to be suspicious; it was true that Mozart could never quite crack the money business – and Constanze didn't help much. Although he was earning a lot – at one stage, at least – Mozart could never save money. It was partly because he was so intent on having a good time! He gave posh dance parties at his apartments, bought a horse, and owned a huge billiards table (he loved billiards, and was a pretty good player). He dressed in the most colourful and fashionable (and therefore expensive) clothes he could find. Constanze's health was a money-draining worry, too; Mozart had to send her off to have pricey cures that he couldn't really afford. It was partly because she was almost always pregnant – six times in eight years; but in the end, only two boys survived. (The Mozarts were rather strange parents, it must be said; when their first-born son was just a few weeks old, Wolfgang and Constanze went off to Salzburg to visit Leopold and Nannerl, leaving the baby in the care of a foster-mother. They stayed in Salzburg for three months; by the time they got back to Vienna, the poor little baby had died! But perhaps this was normal behaviour for those times – or at least for the Mozarts. When Nannerl got married, she had a son, and immediately sent him off to live with the long-suffering Leopold for the next two years. Normal or not, it seems a pretty awful way to treat a child.)

The Mozart apartment must have been very lively – and very

overcrowded. Apart from the Mozarts – with all their music – Mozart's pupils often came to live with their master; then there would be copyists sitting around, busy writing out the parts to Mozart's latest compositions; and to cap it all, the friendly Wolfgang was always inviting visitors to come over. When his guests were there, however, he was often too distracted to talk to them; he would fidget constantly with his napkin at table, or walk up and down the room composing something in his head, completely oblivious to what was going on around him.

Afterwards, when his friends had left, he'd sit down (or stand up – he had a high writing desk made, so that he wouldn't spend his whole life sitting down, crouched over while he wrote), a glass of wine or punch at his side; and he would make his wife tell him everything that had been said that evening, while his hands, seeming to act quite independently from his brain, wrote out the glorious music that he'd created earlier in his mind.

Now, leaving Mozart scribbling away busily, we have to take another (shorter) time-trip; but be prepared – we're going to a sad place. If you don't feel like being depressed, you don't have to come on this bit of the journey; but if you want to know Mozart's tragic fate, fasten that seat-belt...

All his work and worry about money had taken its toll on Mozart's health. Although he was as affectionate as ever to his friends – and particularly to Constanze, of course – and could be as playful and childish as ever, miaowing and prancing around like a maniac, his basically happy nature was eroding; inside, one suspects, he was getting sadder. In 1787, Leopold had died, at the age of sixty-seven – probably muttering to the last about how his son didn't understand people or money, had made the wrong marriage, and would come to a bad end. Mozart had mostly shaken himself free of his father's influence by this time, but he still loved the old stick, and must have missed him a lot. In the following years, Mozart really struggled to make a living – he must have wondered whether Leopold was watching from the other world, a bitter 'I-told-you-so' expression on his ghostly face. What Mozart really wanted was a major post at the Emperor's court in Vienna; but he couldn't get one, partly (it seems) because of the behind-the--scenes plotting of Salieri, an older Italian composer who had a finely paid appointment at the court, and didn't want it threatened. Finally, though, Mozart's career took a turn for the better; in 1791, he was commissioned to write two operas. One was 'The Magic Flute', written for a 'people's theatre' in Vienna, where the tickets were actually affordable; it was an instant hit. The other was called 'La Clemenza di Tito', composed for the Czech capital, Prague, where Mozart's music was adored; he wrote practically the whole opera in eighteen days – half the time it would take most people just to write it out!

But it was just then that Mozart's health started to collapse – dreadful timing. He grew depressed and paranoid, and thought that he was being poisoned. Shortly before this, a strange messenger dressed in black had appeared, and commissioned him to write a 'Requiem', a Mass for the dead; now Mozart became convinced that the messenger came from the other world, and that the 'Requiem' was for himself. (It was actually for a Count, who wished to have a 'Requiem' written for his wife, who'd died recently. He wanted to pretend that he'd composed it himself; but Mozart never knew that.) Mozart didn't finish the 'Requiem', although he worked on it until a few days before he died. After his death, the tragic work was finished by one of his students.

So I'm afraid that this is where our last bit of time-travel has ended: at Mozart's deathbed – and he's still only thirty-five years old! His death was awful. His kidneys failed; his body swelled up, and started to stink horribly. (Ugh – poor Mozart.) He cried bitterly, realising that he was leaving his wife and two sons with no money – just when he felt that his luck was finally about to change. His sister-in-law Josepha Weber had been helping to nurse him; a day before he died, he seemed better, so she went home to her mother. There, as she remembered later, she lit a candle and thought, 'I wonder how Mozart is now?' Just as she thought that, the candle suddenly – for no apparent reason – went out. Full of a horrible premonition, she rushed back to Mozart's bedside – and found that he was really dying. "I have the taste of death on my tongue," he told her sadly. The doctor was sent for, but was in the theatre and wouldn't come until the play was over; when he did arrive, he insisted on putting cold compresses on Mozart's forehead – which gave Mozart such a shock that he lost consciousness, and died a few hours later.

All sorts of horrible things happened then. Constanze was so devastated that she crawled into bed next to the corpse, hoping to catch an infectious disease, and to die herself. (It didn't work.) The next day, a man whose pregnant wife had been Mozart's pupil attacked her with a razor-blade, wounding her, and then killed himself; of course, this started the rumour-factories going overtime, people claiming that the expected child was Mozart's. (It wasn't.) Salieri started to feel guilty and persecuted; many years later, he died in a madhouse, still tormented by accusations that he'd killed Mozart. (He hadn't.)

Mozart's funeral was miserable. At the time, only noblemen and women had grand funerals – most bodies were sent to cemeteries outside Vienna, with three or four corpses to each grave. Mozart's body was taken away, none of his friends or family accompanying it, and laid in just such a grave; and soon, nobody could remember exactly where he was buried – so his remains are lost to us for ever. He deserved better in death – just as he had deserved better in life. It is a tragic story – or at least a story with a tragic ending; and to think what he might have composed, had he lived another thirty-five years!

But still – what we do have is truly miraculous; and we can be grateful that this musical angel came to live amongst us, even for such a short time.

The Music

There has never been a more amazing child prodigy than Mozart; but there have been some that were probably just as amazing. For instance, there was a little English boy, with the rather curious name of William Crotch; he gave his first organ recital when he was two-and-a-half years old! After that, he was dragged around and exhibited, rather like the little Mozart – the difference being that he ended up being just a respectable professor of music. (Actually, he wasn't that respectable; he got fired from his job as head of a music school, because he had a love affair with a student there – ahem. But he was musically respectable, at least.) The real miracle about Mozart was that his music became greater and greater as he got older. Although his childhood compositions are very sweet, and mighty impressive for a child, he would hardly be remembered today if he'd died in his teens. His truly wondrous works date from his twenties and thirties.

Someone once asked Mozart how he managed always to write such perfect music. "I don't know any other way to compose," was the answer. But although every note he wrote was beautiful – Mozart considered that if music wasn't beautiful, it wasn't music – he could express within that beauty any number of emotions or moods, including tragic or even terrifying ones. His music has everything.

Any form suited him: operas, symphonies, concertos, chamber music, religious music, piano sonatas, even dance music; everything that Mozart touched turned to musical gold.

There's something different in his music for everyone: adults, children, musicians, people who've never heard any other music – everybody can love it. His music is like a product of nature, every phrase just the way it has to be. It's difficult to imagine a world without it; in fact, I'd rather not!

What to listen to

Hmm... this is tricky – there's so much that's unmissable! True, there's some unimportant music by Mozart – pieces that he wrote purely to earn money, or when he was really young; but there's also a huge list of masterpieces.

Well, Mozart probably thought of himself primarily as an opera composer, so you might like to begin with a couple of his greatest operas. Maybe you should listen to recordings of them first, so that you get to know them gradually; and then, if you have the chance, go to see them in the theatre. I'd recommend starting with 'Don Giovanni' and 'The Magic Flute'. One of his great achievements as an opera composer is that the music for each character sounds completely different, depending on the nature of the character. For instance, in 'Don Giovanni', the main character, the Don himself, is a charming swine who goes around seducing almost all the women he meets. His music sounds attractive and

powerful – but not very trustworthy.
Eventually, he meets a thoroughly sticky
end when a stone statue comes down
off its pedestal and drags him down to
the flames of hell – it's scary. In 'The
Magic Flute', which is a fairy story of sorts,
you get the wicked Queen of the Night,
whose music sounds quite mad; her
beautiful daughter Pamina, who sounds
pure and innocent; the bird-catcher
Papageno, whose music is bumbling and a
bit silly, but terribly likeable; and so on.
Mozart understood the characters he
created, down to the very last note; and,
good or bad, he gave them the most
beautiful, catchy tunes that any characters
could ever hope for!

Mozart wrote twenty-seven piano
concertos, mostly for his own concerts. Listening to them,
especially the later ones, you can feel what an amazing player he
must have been – and how much he must have enjoyed dazzling
people with his brilliance. (If he felt that someone was really
appreciating him, he'd be happy to play to them for hours.) But you
can also hear how unbearably sad he must have been at times –
and it's often that feeling that stays with you longest. For instance,
try the Piano Concerto no. 23, K488. ('K' stands for 'Köchel', by
the way. Mr. Köchel was a gentleman who spent years cataloguing
all the Mozart pieces he could find – well over 600 of them – and
putting them into the order in which he thought they'd been
written; a huge task.) The three movements of 'K488' are
completely different from each other, yet somehow make up one
satisfying story. The first movement is so elegant, it's as if we've
been transported to a perfect world; in the third, it seems as
though we can hear people laughing and dancing. It's the second

movement, though – the slow movement – that is the heart of the work; it is so sad, that we feel we're looking into a river with no end to its depths. Its beauty is truly magical.

Don't miss the last three symphonies, either – all of them glorious; if I had to choose one, it'd probably be the last, the 'Jupiter' – a feast of golden brilliance. After that, if you're in the mood for totally glorious but tragic music, listen to the 'Requiem', and to the G minor string quintet, K516. And after all those – well, you'll be back for more...

Facts of Life

In 1756, the year Mozart was born, his father Leopold published a book on how to play the violin. It was so good that it's still in print today; nowadays, though, people don't read it to learn how to play the violin, but to find out how violinists used to play in those days ...

Toy story...

As a composer, Leopold is best known today for a work known as the 'Toy Symphony'; for a long time, people thought that it was by Haydn, but we now know that it was written by Leopold. It's a fun piece for orchestra and some toy instruments, such as the quail, the cuckoo and the nightingale. These are very easy to play, so sometimes at special concerts famous people, who aren't really musicians, make guest appearances playing them, just for a lark (or rather, for a quail, cuckoo or nightingale).

Mozart's parents took their choice of names seriously; Mozart's full name was – take a deep breath – Johannes Chrysostomus Wolfgangus Theophilus Mozart. So that they wouldn't waste hours just calling him in for tea, his parents just called him 'Wolfgang' – or 'Woferl' for (even) short(er). Later, Mozart replaced the Greek name 'Theophilus' with one meaning the same ('Beloved of God') in Latin, 'Amadeo'. From about 1770, he made himself sound Italian by calling himself 'Wolfgango Amadeo', and then from 1777 he went a bit French, styling himself 'Wolfgang Amadé'!

Nowadays he's usually referred to as 'Wolfgang Amadeus Mozart'...

What's in a name..?

People have always been fascinated by the rivalry between the rich, but not great, composer Antonio Salieri and the poor genius Mozart. In the 19th century, the famous Russian poet Pushkin wrote a play in verse called 'Mozart and Salieri'; it was later made into a successful opera.

*More recently, the idea was taken up by the British playwright, Peter Shaffer, who wrote the play 'Amadeus', based on the relationship between the two men. This was made into the famous film **Amadeus**. Although the play, and particularly the film, veered miles away from the true facts (Mozart never called himself 'Amadeus', for a start), they made Mozart's*

music more popular than ever; and it is exciting to hear his music blazing out of a cinema screen!

From 1762, when Mozart was just six, Leopold took his family on concert tours that over the next few years would take them to most of the great cities of Europe. These tours took a lot of arranging. The Mozart family would arrive at a town or city and Leopold would immediately get to work, buzzing around discovering who were the most important people in town (if he hadn't found out in advance), and who was most influential at the local court. (Each area was ruled by some prince or princess, who would be surrounded by lots of lesser nobles.)

Then Leopold would take his children to play to these people, who would almost always be gobsmacked. (On the rare occasions that they *weren't* bowled over by his children, Leopold would reason that these people were denying a miracle of God; therefore, they didn't believe in God; therefore, they were bad people; and therefore, their opinion didn't matter. Rather neat, really.) The most influential bigwig might then speak to his important friend, the count; the count might then have a word with his lady-chum, who could be lady-in-waiting to the princess; the princess might then, if she was in the mood, have a word with her husband, the prince. And if the prince wasn't going hunting, he might command the Mozarts to appear at his court, and play for him; and if he was feeling generous that day, and didn't have indigestion or gout or some other ailment that was putting him in a bad mood, the prince might give the family a valuable present. But it was all a bit dicey – there were lots of 'mights'. Another way of presenting the children was to give public concerts, but that involved even more bustling and buzzing on Leopold's part. Meanwhile, the hotel and food bills were rising (even though the Mozarts were very adept at arriving at rich houses just in time for a free lunch); and Leopold didn't like spending money – just earning it. He was a good businessman – but somehow, the Mozarts never got rich...

On the bright side...

Although Mozart's health may have suffered (in the long term, anyway) from this almost constant travelling, his musical education flourished. He loved meeting good musicians. When he was still just eight years old, he made firm friends in London with Bach's youngest son, J. C. Bach (the cheeky one who had referred to his father as 'the Old Wig'). Now a famous composer in his late twenties, J. C. Bach was delighted with Mozart. At a gathering attended by the King and Queen of England, he sat him between his knees at the piano, and the two of them played a game, making up a piece in which one would carry on playing where the other had stopped – and went on for two hours, never getting bored. (I wonder if the King and Queen did?) Around the same time, Mozart stunned some other musicians with his understanding of music. A new work of J. C. Bach's had just been printed and some distinguished grown-ups were sitting and studying it very seriously, while Mozart was (for some reason) rolling around on the table. They showed him the score – and, in a brief pause between rolls, Mozart immediately pointed out a wrong note that nobody else had noticed! (I'm surprised they didn't knock him off the table instantly.)

After 1768, poor Nannerl got left at home with her mother, while Leopold and Wolfgang went off on more tours – principally to Italy, where Mozart first made a real name for himself as an opera composer – in opera's homeland! (Opera was really invented in Italy) Quite an achievement for a teenager...

Talking of achievements...

In Rome, Mozart heard the Pope's choir singing a famous sacred piece, the 'Miserere' by Allegri. This fairly long and complicated work was considered so sacred that nobody was allowed to copy the music. Mozart heard it once, went home, wrote the whole thing out from memory, went to hear it one more time, made a few corrections – and he had a perfect copy of the forbidden piece! If he'd been found out by the Papal authorities, he'd have been in BIG TROUBLE. Those eighteenth-century Italians were a strange lot, it must be said: once, Mozart gave a concert in Naples, wearing a ring. The audience weren't impressed; they were sure that he only played so amazingly because the ring had magical powers. So Mozart took it off, and played without it; and suddenly the audience acclaimed him wildly! Most odd.

After many years of this touring, a problem arose. Leopold's official job was as musician in the service of the Archbishop of Salzburg. The old one had been very free-and-easy about the Mozarts' comings and goings, but he had died; now a new, fiercer Archbishop had been appointed. This one was less impressed by Mozarts in general than his predecessor had been. He pointed out that since Leopold was his employee, and had often been paid his (measly) salary even when he was away, it was high time that he stayed in Salzburg, and earned his daily pumpernickel bread. He didn't seem to notice that Wolfgang was a genius. For the next four years or so, Mozart, much to his disgust, was basically stuck in Salzburg, employed by the Archbishop for a pathetic salary – even less than his father's. After all the excitement of his travelling life, Mozart could hardly bear the boredom of small-town life...

Silly games in Salzburg...

Apart from his composing – which was progressing wonderfully –

and his playing, Mozart had very little to do in Salzburg. All he could do was to fall in love with pretty girls, eat lots of capons, and liver dumplings with sauerkraut (yuk), and play a game with his family and friends in which they made a target – usually a rude picture, extremely rude if Mozart had his way – and then shot at it with an air-rifle! Like an eighteenth-century video-game.

By the time he was twenty-one, Mozart hated the new Archbishop so much that he decided that he couldn't bear to be in the same town as him, and would write asking to be released from his job. The Archbishop responded lovingly – by dismissing both Wolfgang and Leopold. Leopold just couldn't afford to be without his salary, though; so somehow he managed to arrange matters so that he was allowed to stay in his job while Wolfgang got his freedom. He certainly wasn't going to allow Wolfgang to travel by himself. So it was decided that Leopold and Nannerl would stay in Salzburg, while Mozart would be accompanied by his mother on his journey. Having packed all their things for them, arranged as much of their travel as he could in advance, sorted out money arrangements and generally done more of his usual buzzing and bustling, Leopold waved a heart-broken farewell to his wife and son – and settled down to worry...

And Leopold worried about everything...

...whether Wolfgang and his mother were eating the right foods and drinking the right drinks; whether they were

wearing suitable clothes, and putting shoe-trees in their boots;
whether Wolfgang had lice in his hair; whether he would slip on
cobblestones; and so on. And, above all, he worried about money –
or rather, the lack of it. It was ridiculous for him to worry so much
about Wolfgang, who was now a man, and to treat him like a
little child. (Leopold even complained about the fact that the days
were now gone when, every night before going to bed, Wolfgang
would stand on a chair, sing a little song, and kiss his daddy
*again and again on the tip of his nose. A good thing they **were***
gone; Wolfgang would probably have broken the chair by
standing on it, and Leopold would have had to buy a new one.)
The trouble was that, ridiculous or not, Leopold had very good
reasons to worry. In practical ways, Wolfgang was a walking
disaster area. As far as Leopold was concerned, Wolfgang's job was
to earn money. Leopold (who was deeply suspicious of everybody –
'All men are villains,' he declared sweetly) was sure that virtually
nobody else would help him to do so, and that Wolfgang, just by
his brilliance, would make all the other musicians so jealous that
they'd try to spoil his chances. Therefore, he'd have to flatter
everybody, be polite to all the right people, and spend most of his
life being a diplomat. Wolfgang, on the other hand, thought that
his main job was to have a good time and to compose and play
beautiful music. If he did that, he thought, everybody would love
him and help him, and he would make oodles of money, and
become mind-bogglingly famous into the bargain.
Hmm... Unfortunately, Leopold was proved all too right.

Poor Wolfgang – things did not go well for him. First, he fell
madly in love with Aloysia Weber and decided that what he really
wanted to do with his life was to travel around in a coach with
the Weber family, and see if they could somehow earn enough
money to get by. You can imagine what Leopold thought of that.
So Mozart – squiggling and squirming, writing all sorts of half-

truths to his father, trying desperately to win his
mother onto his side – was sternly
ordered by his father to get his neat little
behind off to Paris (mother still in tow)
where he might earn something.
Unwillingly, Mozart did what he
was told and went to Paris, but
he didn't earn anything; and,
to cap a disastrous year, his
mother died there...

Breaking the sad news...

*Mozart may have been immature in many ways – not
surprisingly, perhaps, after his strange upbringing; but when it
came to breaking the news of his mother's death to his father, he
showed his really sensitive side. Although she had in fact already
died, he wrote to his father, telling him only that his mother was
very ill, but that he was hoping for the best. At the same time, he
wrote to a close friend in Salzburg, telling him the whole story,
and asking him to prepare Leopold and Nannerl for the bad news,
and to support them when it arrived. Six days later, he wrote to
Leopold with the sad truth.*

So... with no prospects for making a living in Paris, and feeling
thoroughly lonely and miserable (especially since Aloysia had by
now made it clear that she wasn't interested, thank you very
much) there was no choice for Mozart but to head back to the
dreaded Salzburg, and the 'idiot' (as Mozart politely described
him) Archbishop – who now again employed both Mozarts, for a
yearly salary that would have bought them a few good meals in a
big town. This charmer felt, since they were now safely back on
his payroll, that he had the right to treat both Leopold and
Wolfgang like servants, criticise Mozart's music and even have
their private letters read. (Therefore, if the Mozarts wanted

to write something really private, they wrote it in code; their employer probably chewed his archbishop's hat in frustration, but there was nothing he could do about it). Luckily, after a long eighteen months back in Salzburg, Mozart was commissioned to compose a major opera, 'Idomeneo', to be produced in Munich; this was the break he'd been waiting for. An opera, with its mixture of theatre and music, was just what Mozart was always wanting to write. Of course, he'd written several previously, but this was his first really great one. It was a triumph – even Leopold was happy..!

Music to measure...

*Unlike Bach (see previous chapter) whose music was wholly dedicated to the glory of God (even if he did have to write it to earn a living), or Beethoven (see next chapter) who could only compose when he was so inspired that he couldn't **not** compose, Mozart as a musician was very practical, writing almost exclusively for specific people and occasions.*

*In his operas, he would write music suited to the singers who were going to sing it; he liked to fit the music to the performer, as a tailor fits clothes to the customer. Despite this, he had terrible trouble with temperamental singers. For instance, on the first night of one of his early operas written in Italy, the leading female singer, the 'prima donna', threw a complete wobbly. For a start, the local Archduke and Archduchess arrived three hours late. Then one of the lesser male singers had a dreadful attack of over-acting, which made the audience laugh in the wrong place, and put the prima donna off. And then – probably worst of all – the Archduchess started applauding enthusiastically when the lead male came on. 'Why didn't she applaud like that for **me**?' asked the prima donna* *tearfully, threatening to abandon all future performances.*

It turned out that the lead male had deliberately started a rumour that he was so nervous he wouldn't be able to sing a note unless the Archduchess encouraged him with applause. Mozart had to put up with this sort of thing for his whole life..!

Having received the famous kick on the bum dismissing him from the Archbishop's service, Mozart was a free man. He was kept thoroughly busy in Vienna, people always rushing into his apartment to carry his piano to some palace or hall where he would give a concert and be wildly applauded – but not necessarily rewarded. The money – or rather, the lack of it – was really a problem. Despite all his activity, Mozart found himself in a downward spiral; the more he earned, the more he spent and so the more money he needed. All Leopold's direst predictions came true. Mozart started writing begging letters to his friends; and he had to work harder and harder to make ends meet and to pay back the money he had borrowed; and he often felt horribly empty inside. In his later years in Vienna, his concert engagements dried up; and he found it impossible to get out of debt. He was even sued by a nobleman. A major appointment at court would have helped, but his enemies managed to prevent that. How did he make so many enemies?

Perhaps he was arrogant; he knew how much better a musician he was than anyone else around him (with the exception of Haydn, whom he adored) – and perhaps he made this all too clear to the lesser lights. On the other hand, maybe the others were seething with jealousy just because he *was* so brilliant – scarcely Mozart's fault! Mozart's only permanent appointment was to write background music for the Emperor of Austria's parties, for not very much money – horribly frustrating for him...

So who were his friends..?

Only a few people rallied to Mozart's aid – mostly his fellow Freemasons. The Freemasons were a semi-secret society whose membership consisted of noblemen and the middle classes (like Mozart); their goals were liberty and equality for all men. Towards the end of Mozart's life, it became quite

dangerous to be associated with them, because the Emperor was getting very suspicious of these idealists. But Mozart stuck by them, remaining a Freemason and even getting his father to join them during Leopold's last visit to Vienna – the last time father and son were to see each other. Mozart was passionate about the aims of Freemasonry, and wrote lots of music inspired by it (including his most famous opera, 'The Magic Flute'). He was probably also rather attracted by the good fellowship, the good meals – and all the money that his fellow Masons lent him! On the other hand, maybe his association with the Masons got him into trouble – we really have no idea. In later years, Constanze spoke darkly about having to spend all her time with him to keep him away from bad company. Perhaps she was referring to Masons whose ideas about politics were dangerously free and easy? Or people – possibly Masons – who took advantage of Mozart's generous nature and swindled money out of him? We shall probably never know.

We know about Mozart's sad end; no need to go through all that again. But what happened to his family after his death? Well, of course Constanze was devastated when Mozart died – and broke. How was she going to support herself and the two boys? Happily, lots of people helped her, lending her money, looking after the boys, and arranging concerts for her benefit. Eventually Constanze became quite rich; and she got married again – to a man who wrote one of the first books about Mozart! Of the Mozarts' two sons, one became a civil servant (very civil, I'm sure) and the other a pianist and composer. Curiously, Constanze ended her days living in Salzburg – the town that Mozart couldn't wait to leave! Mozart's sister Nannerl spent her last years there, too, dying in a house just a few feet away from the one in which her brother had been born. It is strange to think of the two old women, who had never really liked each other, both living in the cramped little town, both full of memories of the long-dead genius whom they had loved so much – in their different ways.

In the shadow of his father...

Mozart's pianist/composer son, Franz Xaver Wolfgang, who was only five months old when his father died, was very talented – but the shadow of his great father loomed so large in his life that he never really dared to make the most of his talents; he was always worried about letting down the family name. It's sad that so many people connected with Mozart suffered from being close to him – perhaps they were burnt because they got too close to the sun! We're luckier; today, we can just bask in his glorious rays. And three cities – Salzburg, which he tried to ignore, Vienna, which tried to ignore him, and Prague, the one place where he was truly appreciated in his own lifetime – all make a fortune today from the tourists who flock to any historic building associated with Mozart. There's even a famous chocolate candy named after him – the 'Mozartkugel'. I can imagine what Mozart would have said to that: "How sweet"...

Ludwig van Beethoven

1770-1827

If you had come face to face with Beethoven (pronounced 'Bay-toh-ven') in the streets of Vienna in 1820 – which I admit is unlikely, since you probably weren't born then – you would have thought that he was very odd. His clothes were messy; his hair was messy; his hat was messy. In short, he was a mess. He would walk along very energetically, muttering and gesturing to himself, sometimes breaking into a loud laugh, for no apparent reason. And then he would stop to sing, grunt or howl some notes, whip a notebook out of his pocket, write something down, and stomp off again.

If you had followed him into his rooms, you'd have thought he was even odder. The place was a shambles: sheets of music everywhere, a piano with most of its strings broken and ink spilled inside it, worn-down furniture placed higgledy-piggledy, the remains of half-eaten food lying around; and even possibly – yuk – an unemptied chamber-pot (to put it politely) sitting out in plain view. Lovely. And if, when he came in, he felt too hot after all that energetic walking, he would take a jug of cold water and pour it over his head; it would splash down onto the floor, and through the ceiling of the flat beneath – Beethoven was not a good neighbour to have! Or maybe he would decide to take a bath, and would sit in it for ages, scrubbing himself, singing and growling like a contented bear. After which, he might decide to shave, which would involve lathering soap over his whole face right up to his eyes, because his beard spread right up there; then he'd be bound to cut himself as he shaved, because he was so clumsy. And if he noticed you suddenly and was pleased to see you, you might well find yourself covered with soap too, because he would probably run over and hug you, forgetting where he was or what he was doing, and no doubt knocking over any number of tables or chairs in the process. Then, for good measure, he'd probably crush your hand, taking it into his own hairy paw with a grip so friendly, it would make your eyes water!

However, he might not have noticed you following him down the street and into his rooms at all – because poor Beethoven was deaf! Can you imagine how awful it must have been for a great composer to lose his hearing, never to hear a note of music again?

Try switching on the television, but turning off the sound – and then try to imagine how it would be to feel like that every day of your life. Dreadful – and especially for a musician!

So when you finally looked into his face, you'd see that his eyes were terribly sad; but if you wrote something in his conversation book – which people found was the easiest way to talk to him – and he thought it was funny, you would see his brilliantly white teeth flash into a delighted smile, which might be followed by an enormous laugh that would stretch his whole face – including his already squishy nose – like a rubber mask.

People were often scared of going to meet Beethoven, because the rumour went around that he didn't like people. It's true that if he were busy writing a new piece, he would refuse to see anybody. If he did meet someone he liked, though, he would be wonderfully kind and welcoming. He could be very demanding, and would often become very suspicious of even his closest friends, sometimes behaving very badly to them; but he would almost always feel terribly guilty afterwards, and apologise so miserably that his real friends would forgive him everything. (Once, he wrote to a friend, 'Never come near me again! You are a faithless dog, and may the hangman take all faithless dogs'; the very next day, he wrote to the same friend, 'You are an honest fellow and I now perceive that you were right; so come to see me this afternoon.' A *slight* change of heart!) He behaved the same way to everybody: many aristocratic patrons helped him in lots of ways; Beethoven wasn't ungrateful, but he refused to obey their every wish, just because they'd been born rich. If they wanted to have him as a friend, they had to accept him the way he was – crumpled clothes (he would run away from a house if he was expected to dress up for meals there), rough manners, loud laugh – and quite a temper! He *refused* to be treated like a performing animal. Beethoven didn't like playing in front of people for their pleasure, and hated to be overheard when he was practising or composing; he would play only if he felt like it, and when he was sure that his music was going to be appreciated. Once, he was playing at a posh gathering, while a count was flirting noisily with a pretty girl in an adjoining room. Beethoven suddenly jumped up from the piano and shouted out, "I will not play for such swine!" End of posh gathering.

If someone he knew was in trouble, there was nobody more anxious to help than Beethoven. (One of the people he tried to help was Bach's youngest daughter, Regina Susanna, who by the early 1800s was in sad straits; Beethoven raised money for her.) But as he grew more deaf, although his basically kind nature didn't change, his suspicions became more exaggerated; he was sure that everybody was trying to cheat him in money matters. He imagined that people, especially his housekeepers and servants, were plotting against him, so he would sack them for no good reason – that is, if they hadn't left of their own accord after being shouted at, pelted with rotten eggs and having heavy books thrown at their heads! Also, he kept deciding that the apartment in which he was living was unsuitable in some way or another; and so he was constantly moving house – which meant that his messy rooms became even messier.

The words 'it doesn't matter' don't seem to have been part of his vocabulary at all! *Everything* mattered to Beethoven, from the smallest note in a piece of music to the way he made a cup of coffee. For this (the coffee, not the music) he would insist on sixty beans for each cup – not fifty-nine, not sixty-one, but sixty; he would count them as they went in. It must have tasted horribly strong. Get a grown-up to try making a cup of coffee with sixty beans, and watch their face as they sip it – yuk!

Beethoven was equally passionate about food. Once, he went to a restaurant and ordered a dish; the waiter brought him the wrong one and when Beethoven complained, the man snapped a rude reply and disappeared into the kitchen. A moment later, he re-appeared, carrying lots of plates for the other diners; Beethoven, now thoroughly angry, picked up his meal (which consisted of

meat with lots of gravy) and
threw it into the waiter's face!
The waiter was absolutely
furious, but he was so busy
trying not to drop his
plates, and licking up
the gravy that was
running down his
chin, that there
was nothing
he could do
about it. He
looked so
funny that all the
other diners started
laughing, and suddenly
Beethoven burst out
laughing too, and was in a
good mood again. (I do feel sorry for the waiter, though).

Another time, Beethoven decided that he was fed up with
restaurants, and would cook food himself. He invited some close
friends to dinner and served them with a meal he had made
himself. It was so revolting that none of them could eat any of it;
but Beethoven loved it all, gobbling it up, and completely failed to
notice that his guests were less than delighted!

For some reason, Beethoven is often thought of now as a
scowly, fierce man; but there were many more sides to him than
that. His was a hard fate. As he said himself, "Life is so lovely, but
for me it is poisoned for ever." A lesser man would have been
crushed by the misfortune of losing his hearing, the sense most
vital to his life's activity – but not Beethoven. He was a real hero; I
think it would have been *wonderful* to meet him.

The Music

People often think of his music as scowly, too; but although it is incredibly powerful, and can be dark or even demonic, it can be equally light-hearted, joyous and gentle. Many of Beethoven's pieces reflect his love of nature (such as the lovely 'Pastoral' symphony); much of his music feels as if it belongs outside in the fresh air. There's also lots of humour – Beethoven loved a joke in music as much as in life.

Unlike Bach and Mozart, who seem to have planned their pieces in their heads and (mostly) written them out immediately in fair copies, Beethoven struggled with virtually everything he wrote. He would get an idea for a melody – often when he was out walking – and jot it down in his sketchbook (or anything else that was to hand; if he was at home but had run out of paper, he'd use the window-blinds!) After that, he would work on the idea, changing it, refining it and tussling with it, sometimes for years on end. It's really interesting to look at his sketchbooks, and to see how different some of his most famous tunes would have sounded if he'd let them stand as he first thought of them. Even his final manuscripts usually looked like bombsites. His poor copyists, who had to prepare a fair copy before the piece could be published, had a dreadful time!

Sometimes his life would be obviously mirrored in his music, sometimes not. His famous fifth symphony, written as he struggled to accept his deafness, really sounds like a man defying fate; but his third sonata for cello and piano, written at almost exactly the same time, is one of the most radiant, contented works he ever wrote. As he grew more deaf, his music became even more beautiful; in silence, he created a perfect world of sound. In his last years he wrote some of the most moving music ever composed.

What to listen to

This shouldn't be difficult – there are so many works of complete and utter genius! There are some lesser works by Beethoven – but not many; and all the famous pieces are gigantic achievements. I'd suggest starting with symphonies – perhaps the fifth, with its stormy opening, supposedly depicting fate; or the sixth, the 'Pastoral', in which we can walk through the countryside with Beethoven, hear a violent storm, and then listen to the peasants celebrate as the sun comes out again; or the seventh, which has an amazingly beautiful funeral march as its slow movement. After that, maybe, the piano sonatas – try the 'Pathétique', the 'Moonlight' or the 'Waldstein' sonatas. These works can be your doors to Beethoven's astonishing world – a world that becomes more and more wondrous the more one gets to know it. His music is uniquely satisfying, somehow. Take your time to get to know all his great masterpieces – they'll wait for you! Eventually, you'll come to works like the ninth (and last) symphony – in which, having written eight-and-three-quarter symphonies just for orchestra, he suddenly breaks into song, four soloists and a choir joining the orchestra to sing an 'Ode to Joy'; to his 'Missa Solemnis', the Mass that took him almost four years to write; and to the last string quartets, his profound personal statements that changed the language of music forever. If you make friends with Beethoven, you'll have a companion for life – one who'll never let you down!

Facts of Life

Beethoven was born into a musical family in Bonn in 1770. He was the eldest surviving child of Johann and Maria van Beethoven. His two younger brothers, Kaspar Anton Karl and Nikolaus Johann, were born in 1774 and 1776 respectively. Beethoven was named after his grandfather – and godfather – also called Ludwig (pronounced 'Ludvig') van Beethoven, a well-respected musician at the court in Bonn. Although he died when Beethoven was barely three, little Ludwig retained fond memories of him. Beethoven loved his mother Maria, too; she was quiet and kind – a contrast to his father Johann, who seems to have been a bit of a swine. Johann, also a musician, but less successful than his father, wanted little Ludwig to be as much of a prodigy as Mozart had been, and to make lots of money. Johann used to get very drunk, and force Ludwig to get up in the middle of the night to practise the piano. I'm surprised he wasn't put off music for life!

Nobody really knows...

Nobody knows for certain when Beethoven's birthday was. His birth was registered on December 17th, which probably means that he was born on the 16th; but he might have been born on the 17th – and he himself used to celebrate his birthday on the 15th! For years, he wasn't even sure how old he was – partly because his father, to make him seem more of a prodigy than he was, claimed that he'd been born in 1772. It wasn't until Beethoven was almost forty that he commissioned a friend to find his birth certificate, and found out his true age (well – to within a couple of days, anyway).

Although he wasn't a child prodigy, Beethoven's musical talents had developed impressively by the time he was sixteen; he was already an accomplished pianist and organist, and had composed quite a few works. It was felt that he needed to stretch his musical wings, and he was sent to the great city of Vienna. He had only been there for about two weeks, though, when he received news that his mother was seriously ill, and he hurried back to Bonn.

A meeting with Mozart...

Probably the most memorable event of this brief stay in Vienna was his meeting with Mozart. Mozart, at the height of his fame, listened to Beethoven play a piano piece, but didn't seem terribly impressed. This no doubt annoyed Beethoven, who was said to do his finest improvisations (i.e. composing a piece on the spot) either when he was in a particularly good mood, or when he was really cross. So he launched into an improvisation on a theme that Mozart gave him. Mozart became more and more interested. Finally, he said to some friends who were sitting in the next room, "Keep your eyes on him; some day he will give the world something to talk about."

Beethoven's mother died shortly after his return to Bonn and he was forced to stay in Bonn for the next four years. With his father an increasingly hopeless alcoholic, Beethoven had to replace him as the breadwinner for the family. He was now responsible for the upbringing of his younger brothers – quite a heavy burden for such a young man!

Who'd want to be a violist?

Beethoven's main job during this time was as a violist in the court orchestra. A surprising number of great composers have played the viola (as well as keyboard instruments, in most cases) – including Bach, Mozart and Haydn, as well as many later composers, such as the famous 19th century composers Schubert, Dvorak and Mendelssohn, and the 20th-century composers Benjamin Britten and Paul Hindemith. The viola is a member of the violin family, held under the chin like a violin, but bigger and lower in pitch. I think that these composers enjoyed playing the middle voice in chamber music, so that they could hear everything going on around them. Strangely, these days violas – or rather violists, people who play the viola – are for some reason the butt of lots of jokes, making out (most unfairly) that they're thick. For instance: a violist decides that he is fed up with all these viola jokes, and he's going to take up the violin instead. So he goes into a shop and says, "I'd like to buy a violin, please." The shop-keeper looks at him and says, "I'm sorry, sir, we don't have any in stock. Are you by any chance a viola-player?"

"Er-yes," replies the violist, "how did you know?"

"Because", the shop-keeper points out gently, "this is a fish-and-chip shop".

Haha

Ha?

Well, I thought it was funny...Right – back to Beethoven.

In 1792, the great composer Joseph Haydn (Mozart's old friend) passed through Bonn, where he was shown some of Beethoven's music; he must have been impressed (not surprisingly), for he accepted Beethoven as a student. Later that year Beethoven, generously supported by the Elector of Bonn, followed Haydn to Vienna. This second trip was his chance to leave the comparatively small town of Bonn for ever, and to make his fortune in the big wide world. He was to live in Vienna for the rest of his life – even though he never stopped complaining about the Viennese and their lack of appreciation for his music! Johann died at the end of that year, and Beethoven's two brothers followed him to Vienna; Kaspar Karl became a bank official, Johann Nikolaus a chemist. (Their presence in Vienna wasn't an unmixed blessing for Beethoven, since he constantly quarrelled with them both, and couldn't stand either of his sisters-in-law.) Having arrived in the great city, Beethoven was prepared to work as hard as he needed to become a great musician; but his studies with Haydn weren't a great success – Beethoven can't have been easy to teach! He managed to make a reputation for himself fairly quickly, though, both as a pianist and as a composer. He gave many concerts for the music-loving aristocracy of Vienna, some of whom employed private orchestras and even opera companies. He also had to teach to earn a living; not a *great* idea. He used to get horribly frustrated with his pupils – so much so, that he bit one of them on the shoulder! In later years, three noblemen in Vienna gave him an annual salary so that he wouldn't have to worry too much about money and could devote all his time to writing the music he wanted to write. (Beethoven went on worrying anyway. He was always worried about money, and didn't know how to spend it wisely; and it didn't help

when, shortly after they'd promised him the salary, one of the noblemen was killed in a riding accident, and another was declared bankrupt!)

What sentimental fools!

Beethoven's early concerts would have been very different from the concerts we have today. For a start, most of them would not have been given in concert halls, but at the grand residences of princes, counts and so on; the audience, consisting only of upper-class ladies and gentlemen, would all have been specially invited. Beethoven would sometimes perform works by other composers, such as Bach or Mozart, and would also introduce his own newest compositions; but he was probably most famous at this time for his improvisations. Someone would give him a theme, and he would immediately develop it into a whole piece. He was so amazing at this, that he could easily move his listeners to tears; but if he noticed them crying, he was liable either to laugh at them, or to get really annoyed and accuse them of being sentimental fools! Occasionally another 'virtuoso' (i.e. brilliant) pianist and composer would come to Vienna and be a huge success. If Beethoven thought another musician was good, he'd be wonderfully friendly to him or her; for instance, when he met the well-known composer Weber (cousin of Mozart's wife Constanze) he took him by surprise by hugging him repeatedly before they were even introduced, informing Weber that he was 'a devil of a fellow'! But if he didn't think much of the newcomer, he'd say so in no uncertain terms, and might have to prove that he was the champ. Once, such a person came from Paris and played a quintet he'd written, plus an 'improvisation' (perhaps not so improvised) on a theme that Beethoven had used in one of his compositions. Beethoven took this as an insult; slouching his way towards the piano, he grabbed the cello part of the upstart's quintet, put it upside down on the piano's music-stand, hammered out a few notes from it with one finger, and from these notes constructed such a breathtaking fantasy that his audience was left gasping – and there was no sign of his 'rival', who'd stormed out in a fury. Ha!

By the time he was thirty, Beethoven was forced to admit to his closest friends that he was going deaf. He had a huge ear-trumpet made for him by his friend Maelzel (who also developed the metronome, a ticking device that we still use today to help us keep time in music); but even that didn't help. In 1802, he wrote a will, in the form of a deeply tragic note to his brothers, telling them how he had suffered from his affliction. Written in a little village some way away from Vienna called Heiligenstadt (Beethoven used to spend several months each year in the countryside), the letter is known as 'the Heiligenstadt Testament'. His hearing gradually became worse and worse, until all he could hear was a constant roaring and whistling; and eventually, for the last nine years of his life, he could hear almost nothing at all – just silence.

Because of his deafness...

...Beethoven had to phase out his public appearances as a pianist; he could no longer hear whether he was playing the right notes. He continued conducting his own orchestral compositions, though, almost to the end of his life; but this led to some very embarrassing moments. He'd probably never been a great conductor anyway, and after he lost his hearing, he became a downright disaster. Being Beethoven, everything was done with

exaggerated gestures. If he wanted the orchestra to play softly, he was likely to creep right underneath his music-desk; if he wanted them to play a loud chord, he'd suddenly leap right into the air. Sometimes, because it was difficult for him to tell what the orchestra was playing, he'd get lost and would go leaping into the air right in the middle of a beautiful soft passage! Oh dear...

Beethoven never married, but he certainly had 'an eye for the ladies'; in fact, he often had *four* eyes for the ladies, because when he saw an attractive woman passing in the street, he'd whip out his spectacles and examine them closely as they walked by. (I'm surprised he didn't get his face slapped!) He was always falling madly in love, and proposed to several women; but for various reasons, it never worked out. Some of them rejected him because they thought he was mad; some were married already; and some did actually fall in love with him, but they were from aristocratic families, who wouldn't let them marry a mere composer! Actually, there was quite a bit of confusion about that; if a German name has the prefix 'von', it means that the person is from an aristocratic family, whereas the prefix 'van' is quite common in Holland. Beethoven had Dutch ancestors, which explains the 'van'. Some snobby people thought that he was called Ludwig von Beethoven and were very disappointed when they found out his real name. A rubbishy rumour went around that the true explanation for his genius was that he was the illegitimate son of King Frederick the Great! I wonder what Beethoven's mother would have thought about that?!

A love letter...

Among the papers Beethoven left behind after his death was a letter he had written which has become famous as the letter to 'the Immortal Beloved'. It is a wonderfully passionate letter to a woman whom he obviously adored and, judging from the

*intimate tone of the letter, seems to have adored him too.
Although there are many theories, nobody knows for sure who 'the
Immortal Beloved' really was – an intriguing mystery.*

Beethoven was stuck in Vienna when it was occupied by the
French army in 1805. He was terrified by the bombs (perhaps
they were particularly painful for his troubled ears?) and would
rush to his brother Caspar Carl's cellar and bury his head in
cushions down there to block out the noise. It was just a week
after the French had marched in that Beethoven's only opera,
which he called 'Leonore', was first performed – lousy timing!
Most of his supporters had hastily removed themselves to the
safety of the country, so the opera didn't have much of an
audience – or much of a success. Later, one of Beethoven's tame
princes called a conference at his house at which many people
from the arts suggested to Beethoven how he might improve the
opera. Beethoven went into a major sulk – not surprising, really;
but eventually he made a lot of changes, including writing four
completely different overtures before he was satisfied, and
changing the name of the opera to 'Fidelio' (pronounced 'Fid-
eh-leio'). Eventually, it was accepted as one of the greatest of all
operas.

Losing his temper with the Emperor...

*The French army was headed by the famous Napoleon. At first,
Beethoven was very impressed by Napoleon, who had risen from
humble beginnings to become the most powerful man in Europe.
Beethoven considered that all men were born equal (which is why,
when he brought voices into his ninth symphony, he chose a text
with the basic message that 'All men are brothers') and was
suspicious of the idea of aristocrats, even though they supported
him. So he liked the thought of the 'lowly born' Napoleon
becoming ruler of the French, without having a fancy title.
Beethoven planned to dedicate his third symphony, later known*

as the 'Eroica', to Napoleon; but then Napoleon had himself crowned Emperor of France. Beethoven was livid, "So now he will tread all the rights of man underfoot to indulge his own ambition!" he shouted. He took the title-page of the symphony with the dedication, tore it in half and hurled it to the floor. A copy of the symphony still exists with Napoleon's name viciously scratched out – it's quite a startling sight!

In 1815, Beethoven's brother Casper Carl died and appointed Beethoven to be the guardian of his nine-year-old son Karl; unfortunately, he asked him to share the responsibility with the boy's mother Johanna – and she and Beethoven hated each other. 'God permit them to be harmonious for the sake of my child's welfare,' wrote Caspar Carl in his will. Fat chance. A huge struggle ensued, which went on for years and involved Beethoven in a vast amount of legal wrangling. This may have been the darkest period in Beethoven's life. He was so obsessed with the battle for little Karl that he found it hard to compose anything for almost two years.

But for Karl...

...life wasn't easy, either; torn between his overbearing uncle and his manipulative mother, he became completely confused and miserable. Eventually, in 1826, Karl tried to shoot himself with two pistols; luckily, he was a lousy shot, and survived with fairly minor injuries. Beethoven was devastated, probably realising that his jealousy and possessiveness towards Karl had been a large factor in Karl's unhappiness; a friend saw Beethoven shortly

after the incident, and said that he looked like a seventy-year-old. Still, at least Karl survived; and when Beethoven died, Karl inherited his entire estate. In his impossible, larger-than-life way, Beethoven really loved the boy.

From 1817, Beethoven threw himself back into composing with a vengeance. From the last ten years of his life came some of his greatest works – some of the greatest music ever written, in fact. These include his last three piano sonatas, the ninth symphony and the 'Missa Solemnis'; and, last of all, a series of string quartets that sum up his lifetime of joy, suffering and resignation. Although many people found Beethoven's extraordinary late music hard to understand – it was light-years away from the music of most of his contemporaries – it was generally realised that he was the greatest composer alive. At one of his last concerts, in 1824, he conducted the first performance of the ninth symphony and three movements from the 'Missa Solemnis'. At the end, he stood leafing through the score, until one of the singers pulled at his sleeve and pointed behind him; he turned round and realised that the audience was standing up and cheering him. Beethoven hadn't heard a thing.

A living memory...

*It all seems so long ago – Beethoven died in 1827, after all. But a little story seems to me to bring it all much closer: my father, who was born in Russia in 1917, was taken to live in Vienna in 1923. He still has a vague memory of going to see an apartment there, and of meeting a 102-year-old landlady, who ruffled his hair. My grandfather recognised the address of the apartment-building. "Wasn't this one of the houses where Beethoven lived towards the end of his life?" he asked. The old landlady looked disgusted. "Ach!" she exclaimed, "I remember him very well; he was a filthy old man – he used to spit all over the floor!" Hmm... well, it's true that he did have an unfortunate habit of spitting out of the window, and often missed, or thought that the mirror was the window; but still – not exactly a **beautiful** story to remember him by. At least my father met someone who had met Beethoven, though; and somehow that seems to bring the great man (Beethoven, I mean, not my father!) much nearer to our time.*

In late 1826, Beethoven, his basically strong constitution weakened by many years of illness, caught a nasty chill; he couldn't shake it off, and he became weaker and weaker. One really nice thing happened to him on his deathbed, at least: the Royal Philharmonic Society of London, hearing of his condition, sent him £100 – a great deal of money in those days – to relieve him of money worries. Beethoven was thrilled; but it was one of his last happy moments. He died on March 26th, 1827, during a violent thunderstorm. It was said that the people around his bed saw him illuminated by lightning, sitting up and shaking his fist at the heavens, before sinking down onto his pillows for the last time.

A final goodbye...

There were only about 250,000 people living in Vienna at that time – roughly thirty-two times fewer than the population of London or New York today. At Beethoven's funeral, a huge crowd lined the streets to say farewell to the great master. It's thought that around 20,000 people showed up – the equivalent of around 640,000 people in London or New York these days! Pretty impressive, really...

Robert Schumann

1810-1856

Robert Schumann ('Shoeman') is one of my all-time heroes; I love him! I love his music; I love his writings; and I love his character. But I'd have hated to have lived in the same house as him; he was *impossible*! The trouble with him was that he was never normal; either he was so happy that he could hardly speak, or so depressed and miserable that he couldn't speak at all. In fact, speaking in general wasn't his strong point. Once, for instance, he wanted his new symphony performed, so he went to see his friend Ferdinand David, a violinist and conductor. The two men sat opposite each other in silence for an hour or so, while poor Mr. David tried to guess what it was that Schumann wanted. When he finally guessed, he agreed to perform the symphony; Schumann was delighted, and made gestures to show that he'd willingly pay the musicians himself. Having been that communicative, he obviously felt he'd done his bit; he sat back in silence, smoked two cigars (Schumann loved cigars), tried to say something (but nothing came out because he kept wiping his hand over his mouth at the crucial moment) and then got up to leave. He took his hat, left his gloves behind, nodded, went to the wrong door, couldn't get out, panicked, found the right door and vanished – probably leaving Mr. David wondering what planet his visitor had come from!

Although he was basically very good-looking – at least when he was young – Schumann looked most odd at times. When he composed, he liked to smoke cigars; but the smoke got into his eyes, and he didn't like that at all. So he'd push his mouth forward as far as possible, so that the smoke went off in front of him. He liked to whistle or hum the notes he was composing, but that was difficult to do with a cigar in his mouth, and his mouth all pushed out; so he'd end up making strange noises and even stranger faces – again like a creature from another planet.

Actually, he *was* almost on another planet, or at least in another world, most of the time. He found it hard to notice what was going on in real life, because his head was so full of his dreams, his fantasies, his poetry. He loved books as much as he loved music; his favourite books tended to be novels about characters in weird masks, people who saw themselves transformed into frightening shapes, lovers who refused to be parted, even by death. He was what we call a 'romantic artist' – everything he wrote, or even thought, somehow seemed to come from another world that was more beautiful, more dramatic, more magical, than our own. Strangely enough, though, he was startlingly practical in some ways. For instance, he kept household books in which he would note down every penny he earned or spent, with strict accuracy; he was a really curious mixture.

Perhaps he inherited this combination of romantic dreams and precise detail from his father, August Schumann. August was a publisher, bookseller and writer; the books he wrote range from novels full of unearthly mystery and love, to something called 'Address Book' – a book listing the addresses of all the businesses in his region of Germany. It's funny to think of Schumann's father having compiled an early version of the 'Yellow Pages'!

August died when Schumann was sixteen, and he was left to the tender care of his mother. She was no doubt very well-meaning; but she was also a bit of a pain. She had all Schumann's depressive tendencies, but none of his creative fire and explosive energy. Everything Schumann did tended to make the poor woman take to her armchair in tears. At first, she forced him to study law, even though he was desperate to become either a writer or a musician. (She worried that he'd never be able to earn a living without a 'proper' profession.) Then, when he was nearly nineteen, Schumann met a piano-teacher called Friedrich Wieck (pronounced 'Veak'), who told both Schumann and his mother that he could teach Robert to become a great pianist. This sent Mrs. Schumann into her armchair for days on end; but eventually she gave in. Afterwards, when Robert actually went to live in Wieck's house and submitted to his teacher's fierce discipline, it was back to the armchair for his mother, who didn't think it was right for her Robert at all. Even when Robert wrote her a happy letter, it would remind her of how sad the last one had been, or how sad she was by comparison – and so it'd be back once more into the armchair for Mrs. Schumann...

Mind you, Wieck *was* a bit much. Perhaps it would be too simple to say that he was a thoroughly nasty piece of work; but he certainly wasn't a thoroughly *nice* piece of work. He had a daughter named Clara, who was eleven years old when Schumann went to live in her father's house; she was already a brilliant pianist, and her father's pride and joy. Wieck also had a son named Alwin, who was nine; he was a violinist, but considerably less brilliant than his sister. One day, Alwin played to his father, rather badly; Wieck knocked him to the floor, pulled his hair and yelled at him. Clara, smiling quietly, just sat herself at the piano and started to play, perfectly as usual. Schumann, who witnessed this, was utterly shocked; 'Am I among human beings?' he wondered.

On the other hand, Wieck was sometimes very nice to Schumann; and Clara was even nicer. When Schumann went out for walks, he'd be staring at the sky, full of his usual dreams about the flowers and trees, the birdies and the bees (well – maybe a *bit* more poetic than that!); Clara would walk behind him, looking at the ground – and whenever she saw a big stone ahead, she'd tug at the back of Schumann's shirt to warn him. A good arrangement – for him, anyway...

And then a strange thing happened: Clara grew up. Suddenly, Robert noticed that she'd become a bit of all right to look at – and one day, he kissed her passionately. (Apologies to those who don't like this sort of thing – you can always skip to the next bit. I once took my son to an adventure film: I was worried that the violent scenes might upset him, but he didn't seem bothered at all. Then a kissing scene came up, and he spent the next five minutes covering his eyes and groaning. It's the wrong way round, really – but let it pass.) Anyway – Clara nearly fainted (good thing she didn't; they were on some stone steps at the time, and she might have hit her head, and ruined the whole thing). She fell madly in love with Robert, and he with her, and all was rosy and wonderful.

Except for one thing – Wieck. He did his *nut!* He wanted his daughter to be the most famous pianist in the world, to tour around making huge fees (which he'd keep) and eventually maybe get married to some prince – so long as the prince were rich. Marriage to this young whippersnapper Robert Schumann, who didn't have much money, drank too much (Schumann was rather addicted to champagne, and to beer – and to the two of them mixed up together – yuk!) and was altogether too weird for words, was definitely *not* on the menu. So he forbade the lovers to see each other.

Schumann wasn't the type to take such things lightly. Not for him the 'oh well, can't have Clara, better luck next time' attitude. He plunged into deep misery; and to cap it, he was so desperate to improve as a pianist that he invented a finger-strengthening machine that actually ruined his hand – and he couldn't play the piano any more! On the other hand (so to speak), both his composing and his writing were really starting to take off. Earlier, his writing had usually consisted of rather awful stories about skeletons, graveyards and pale young maidens running around in the dark in their nighties; and his music had often sounded a bit like the soundtrack to the stories. But now he'd started up a distinguished musical newspaper, and was writing strange-but-brilliant articles about music that were making him famous as a critic. And he was pouring his feelings of love for Clara into a series of glorious pieces for the piano – the instrument that she played so brilliantly, and that he would never really play again.

Poor Clara was torn between her bullying father, who'd been her only influence for years (her mother had, understandably, run off with another man some time ago), and the neurotic but lovable Robert. Sometimes she decided that one was right, sometimes the other. Since they weren't allowed to meet, she and Robert wrote to each other constantly. Some of her letters said that she loved Robert, she couldn't live without him; then he'd be so happy he'd have to write a new piece of music, full of secret messages for her. In some of her other letters, though, she worried that Robert wouldn't make enough money to keep them both, that his music was too hard for audiences to understand, that she couldn't abandon her father. Of course, Robert would take her point calmly and reasonably; he'd just threaten to kill himself. Eventually, the situation became so unbearable that the lovers took Wieck to court, and asked the law to give them permission to marry. They won the case, Wieck went on the sulk for years on end, and it was wedding-bells time for Robert and Clara. He was thirty; her twenty-first birthday was the day after the wedding. All in all, they had quite a lot to celebrate! Or so it seemed.

The young couple's marriage started out ecstatically; but there were soon problems, problems. The main one was that Clara wanted to keep giving concerts, and Robert wanted her to stay at home, have children, and look after them and him. It must have been horribly frustrating for her – one of the greatest pianists in the world (and a very talented composer as well), not allowed to travel and perform, not even allowed near the piano while her husband was composing (which was sometimes all day long), because the noise distracted him. It wasn't much fun for him, either; of course, he felt guilty about being so selfish – but he needed a quiet life in his home if he was going to achieve anything at all. He hated travelling, and couldn't compose at all when he was away; also he did not enjoy at all being treated as an unnecessary extra to his famous wife – and yet it just wasn't done in those days for a wife to travel without her husband. What were they to do?

Well, somehow they managed; but she was usually frustrated, and he was often terribly depressed. They stayed together, however, and had seven children (only one of whom died really young – survival rates had improved since the days of Bach and Mozart); and at times Robert and Clara were very happy.

Schumann was becoming even odder, though. At the age of forty, he was appointed for the first time to a proper position: music-director in the town of Düsseldorf. Nice in theory – a disaster in practice. For a start, he had to conduct the local orchestra and choir; and conducting, showing other people how to play, was never going to be his strong point. He'd go off into a dream in the middle of a piece, and the performance would grind to a halt; he'd complain that the horns were playing too softly, and somebody would have to tell him gently that actually the horns hadn't played a note, because he'd forgotten to show them where to come in. He'd keep dropping his baton (the little stick with which conductors beat time); eventually he had to tie it around his wrist – it must have looked most peculiar! He was also supposed to be a man-about-town, on friendly terms with all the local bigwigs; forget it – not Schumann's style at all. He was finding it harder and harder to talk to people; he would sit there with his lips pursed up in a silent whistle, seemingly not noticing that someone was trying to speak to him. So perhaps it's not surprising that the people of Düsseldorf decided that their lovely town would be still lovelier without Schumann as music director; and they told him they wanted him out. Schumann was livid – and so was Clara; and basically it was catastrophe, gloom and doom all round.

One day around this time, though, something really nice happened: a young man came to visit them – and the whole Schumann family fell in love with him. The children loved him, because he would suddenly start doing extraordinary acrobatic feats on the stairs above them, leaping from bannister to bannister, and making them gasp with amazement. Their parents loved him too – Robert because the young man was an amazing composer and as full of poetic fantasy as he himself had been at that age, Clara because he was an amazing composer ... and an amazingly good-looking one, too. His name was Johannes ('Yohannes') Brahms ('Brahms' – well, I don't know a clearer way of spelling it!) and he was to become one of the greatest of all composers – so great, in fact, that he gets the whole next chapter to himself. At this point, though, he was just beginning; and Schumann was the first to recognise his genius. In return Brahms, and the mutual friend who had introduced him to the family, the famous violinist Joseph Joachim ('Yoachim', 'ch' as in Bach), were to be great friends to the Schumanns in times of trouble; and big trouble was brewing.

A painter made sketches of both Brahms and Schumann around this time. Brahms is extremely handsome, sensitive and almost baby-faced. At twenty years old, his voice hadn't yet broken properly, and he hardly had to shave. Schumann, by contrast, looks thoroughly disturbing: he is fat, his eyes are a very strange shape, and he looks bewildered. (At the bottom of the picture is inscribed the violin part from the beginning of the slow movement of his first piano trio – one of the saddest things he ever wrote, like a portrait in sound of depression and loneliness.) His oddness was becoming more than just eccentricity; he now started to hear voices in his head. Sometimes they sang beautiful music; once he got up in the middle of the night, convinced that angels had dictated a glorious melody to him. He wrote it down, and started to write a piece based on the melody. It's a touching, gentle piece, filled with the sadness of parting; but it's strange that he didn't notice that the 'angelic' melody was one he'd composed himself years before, and had re-used since.

The dreadful truth was that he was going mad. Sometimes the voices in his head would turn nasty, telling him that he was a wicked sinner, a terrible composer; they would play him horrible music. He worried that he would do something violent to Clara, in a fit of insanity; and although he was carefully watched, one day he managed to slip out of the house and down to the river that flows through Düsseldorf, the Rhine (which had inspired one of his most famous works, the 'Rhenish' symphony). Almost twenty years earlier, during a quarrel with Clara, he had threatened to throw the engagement ring she'd given him into the Rhine, and himself after it; now he carried out this terrible threat. First he threw in his wedding-ring – at least, that's presumably what happened; although nobody saw him do it, the ring was certainly lost from that day, and never found. What happened next we do know: Schumann clambered over a row of boats that made a bridge across the river – and plunged into the icy water. Some fishermen had spotted him, and rushed to pull him out. He tried to throw himself back in, but they were stronger than he was; and eventually they led him home, threading their way through a group of people celebrating a carnival. (Again, one of his most famous pieces is called 'Carnival', a joyous work for piano; what a sad irony!) Once home, he settled down a bit, and even finished the variations that he'd started a few days earlier on the 'angelic' melody; but he was really in despair. Finally, he made up his mind; he was going to a mental asylum. Clara begged him not to leave her; but he told her that he had to, that he would soon come back cured.

So, flanked by two attendants and a doctor, Schumann climbed into a horse-drawn carriage, and left his house without saying goodbye to Clara, or to his children, whom he would never see again. He went to an asylum quite a long way away from Düsseldorf, at a little place called Endenich, near Bonn (the city where Beethoven had been born). When he arrived, he was in a terrible state, convinced that his wife was dead, shouting till he was hoarse, and sure that he was the victim of a plot. Over the next few months, though, he calmed down and improved considerably. In time, he felt that he was ready to go home – but, although he'd asked to be put in the asylum to start with, he soon discovered that it was a different matter to get out of it. For a start, even though he was much better, he wasn't exactly normal – he'd *never* been normal; and he still had relapses into  madness. So the doctors tut-tutted, and examined what he produced in the bathroom each day, and conferred – and decided that he wasn't well enough to leave.

What a terrible situation for everyone! Clara must have felt horribly guilty; her feelings were complicated, to say the least. She couldn't visit Schumann; at least, the doctors strongly advised against it. She was (presumably) longing for Schumann to 'come back cured', as he had promised her that he would; but at the same time, she may have been worried that Schumann would turn violent if he was let out of the asylum too soon. Also, she was now able to travel around giving concerts, which is what she'd always wanted to do – and that would have to stop if Schumann were to come home. And there was an added complication: she had fallen in love with Brahms – and he with her. As for Brahms, he must have felt dreadful: he was devoted to Schumann, and was one of the few who were allowed to visit him occasionally – but he was in love with Schumann's wife. What a dreadful mix of emotions!

But it was worst of all, of course, for Schumann. He was abandoned, living by himself in two small rooms, cut off from his family, his friends and from music – from life, in fact. He described himself as 'Robert Schumann – Honorary Member of Heaven' – a living dead man. He did compose quite a bit – mostly Bach-inspired fugues, which had always helped him organise his mind; but afterwards he would tear the music up, convinced that it was worthless. From time to time he would play on a piano in the asylum; but one person who listened and reported on it thought that it was dreadful – like a broken machine that still tries to work, but can only produce spasms. Occasionally he would get violent, shouting and threatening to throw a chair at his attendant; often it was impossible to understand what he was trying to say – his speech, never his strong point, deteriorated to the point of gibberish. If he wasn't writing fugues, he would try to order his mind by listing place-names from maps in alphabetical order. (Perhaps he remembered his father's old book of 'Addresses'?) He'd get so obsessed with this, that he'd ignore anyone who came to see him; in fact he was no longer able to communicate with people.

Eventually, he must have realised that he was never going to be able to leave the asylum; and he gave up. His physical health collapsed, he stopped eating, his limbs started to twitch uncontrollably. He was dying. Finally, after two-and-a-half years, Clara came to visit him, accompanied by Brahms. Schumann recognised Clara; she hardly recognised him. With a huge effort, he tried to put his shaking arm around her, and made an attempt to smile. Babbling incoherently, he managed the word 'my' – did he mean 'my Clara'? He sucked wine and jelly off her fingers, when he would have refused it from anyone else. But it was all too late; he died the next day, at a time when no-one was with him. The attendant came into his room to see how he was – and found him dead. All alone, even at the last moment.

It's such a sad story that I can hardly bear to think of it. The only possible consolation is the thought that when he was happy, he was wildly, ecstatically happy – probably far happier than you or I will ever be. And it's nice to think, too, how glad (and possibly surprised) he would have been to see how people all over the world respond to his music today – to see how close they feel to his passionate heart.

The Music

To speak very generally, I would say that Bach's music shows us God's view of the world; Mozart's music is like a part of nature; Beethoven speaks for all mankind; and Schumann? Schumann's music tells us what it was like to be Robert Schumann; and yet it still speaks to us all, because his emotions were so strong, so real, that we can recognise ourselves in him. Everything that he experienced in his life comes pouring through his music; there is no composer whom we get to know as intimately as we get to know him. He tells us his deepest secrets, shares with us his most private dreams – in fact, he talks to his listeners as if we were his most beloved friends.

This is partly because most of his music was written especially for those closest to him – most often for Clara. Often the music stops suddenly, and a quote from one of Schumann's earlier works will be heard (or from a work by another composer whom they both loved) – a personal message for Clara, which she will have understood perfectly. There is also the feeling with Schumann that he was not writing to order, like Bach and Mozart had to, or because, like Beethoven, he had to scale a mighty peak; Schumann composed because he *had* to, because the inspiration was so strong inside him that if he hadn't let it come out, he would have exploded! Often, he would write incredibly quickly; and it was impossible to predict what he would compose next. To start with, he wrote lots of huge works for piano; then, in the year he married Clara, he suddenly became inspired to write songs – and wrote more than 140 of them that year! Two years later, he became interested in chamber music, and wrote five great works in just over six months. The trouble with this sort of inspiration was that when he was composing he would go into a feverish hive of activity; when he finished, he'd come tumbling down into a lethargic, depressed state.

How can I describe the beauty of the music? Schumann takes us to places we could never have found without him. Sometimes his music is so peaceful and gentle that we feel we are in heaven; at other times, it is so fierce and frightening that it is as if we are in some sort of hell. It all depends on what sort of dream he is having.

Once, Clara told him that he reminded her of a child; soon after that, he started on a series of pieces for and about children that he continued writing until almost the end of his creative life. Often young pianists play his 'Album for the Young', two books of piano pieces that start out quite easily for the performer, and become more difficult as they go along, but never get too hard for talented children to play; all the pieces are magical. Older pianists love to play his 'Scenes from Childhood'; these are quite demanding for the pianist, but conjure up lovely images of children – 'Dreaming', 'Strange Story', 'Perfect Happiness' – and so on. Then there is the famous series of much larger works for the piano, such as 'Carnival' and 'Kreisleriana'; they are all full of love-poems, portraits, strange jokes, and sadness mixed with joy – like nothing else written before or since.

Songs suited Schumann perfectly, with their mixture of poetry and music; his are irresistible – each song conjures up a whole world of feeling and pictures. His four symphonies are wonderful, too; the first, the 'Spring', starts with an ecstatic fanfare – what a great way to start your first symphony! And so on – everything he wrote is lovable, curious, individual; of course, his cello concerto is one of my all-time favourite pieces of music – not surprisingly...

As Schumann grew older and stranger, his music, naturally,

became stranger too. There are people even now who say that his late music is weak and uninspired. I think these people should all be pelted with elderberries and have ducks' eggs broken over their silly heads. His late music isn't weak; it's just that he wanders down some curious paths, and it's up to us to follow him. If we do, we'll find landscapes as beautiful as ever – they're just different; the music is always worth the extra effort that it demands.

I do hope that you'll get to know and to love Schumann's music; through it, you'll get to know his soul – and it's a wonderful soul!

What to listen to

A good beginning to your friendship with Schumann might be the exciting 'Piano Quintet,' for piano, two violins, viola and cello; or the wonderful piano concerto, full of romantic passion, written for Clara. Then you can move on to the symphonies, perhaps starting with the first, the 'Spring', or the third, the 'Rhenish' – they're thrilling! To go deeper into the more intimate side of his music, listen to his songs: try the song-cycles (i.e. sets of songs) 'Dichterliebe,' or 'Liederkreis' – following the texts of the poems, which are beautiful. (They're in German, but most recordings should have a little booklet with English and French translations, as well as the original words.) If you want to explore Schumann's darker creations, try his first piano trio, for violin, cello and piano, op. 63; and his 'melodramas', op. 122 (very scary poems, read by a speaker, with piano accompaniment by Schumann). And then, if it doesn't make you feel too sad, listen to his last piece, the gentle set of variations in E flat for piano, op. post., on the 'angels' theme – the piece now often called the 'geister', or 'spiritual', variations; this was his sublime farewell to the world. These are just entry-points to his world, though – there's so much more that you'll love...

Facts of Life

Schumann – full name Robert Alexander Schumann – was born in a little town in Eastern Germany called Zwickau, on June 8th, 1810.

Today...

Zwickau is officially known as 'Robert-Schumann-Stadt', German for 'Robert Schumann City'; Schumann would have been amazed!

The town where Wieck lived when Schumann met him and Clara, and where Schumann settled for fourteen years from the time he was twenty, was Leipzig – where Bach had spent his last twenty-seven years.

A true friend...

When Schumann had been in Leipzig for a few years, a great composer, pianist and conductor called Felix Mendelssohn arrived to take over the local concerts. Schumann hero-worshipped him – and Mendelssohn was good to Schumann, conducting his symphonies, defending him against Wieck, and appointing Schumann to teach at the new school of music in Leipzig. The only real hint of trouble between them arose when Clara and Mendelssohn got a little too friendly for Schumann's liking; but it passed. Schumann was heart-broken when Mendelssohn died suddenly at the age of thirty-seven. Schumann's last son – whom he never saw – was named Felix, in honour of Mendelssohn. (Incidentally,

*Mendelssohn appears somewhere on my family tree; I'm very
proud of that – even though I did absolutely nothing to make it
happen!)*

The newspaper that Schumann founded in Leipzig, 'The New
Musical Journal', not only made Schumann famous; his generous
and wise reviews of other composers' music made several of
them famous in Germany. He was one of the few critics about
whom musicians didn't feel (to quote a famous remark) like
lamp-posts feel about dogs!

Split personality...

*Schumann decided that the best way to cope with his extremes of
mood was to think of his personality as two different people; he
invented two imaginary 'companions' called Florestan and
Eusebius ('You-say-be-us'). They were opposing characters,
Florestan outgoing and passionate, Eusebius thoughtful and
inward-looking. Schumann used them when writing his reviews –
he would describe their 'conversations' about new pieces; they also
crop up in his piano pieces – Florestan in the extrovert bits,
Eusebius in the introvert bits. Schumann really lived in a fantasy
world!*

When he was thirty-four, Schumann slid into such a depression
that he and Clara decided that a change was needed. He sold the
newspaper, and they moved to the city of Dresden. The strange
thing about moving to Dresden was that almost the only person
they knew there was – the dreaded Wieck! Although Wieck had
become friendlier now that Schumann was more successful as a
composer, he wasn't exactly their favourite person. No wonder
Schumann was often ill and miserable during the five years he
spent there; still, he did compose a huge amount in that time –

including his only opera, a fascinating tale of good and bad magic called 'Genoveva.'

Night-time rescue...

The most dramatic thing that happened to the Schumanns in Dresden was probably the revolution of 1848. There was lots of fighting near their house; men were shot and lay dead in the streets. Clara decided that it was time for them to escape, so, leaving the younger children in the care of a nanny, she took the oldest, Marie, and Robert to a nearby village, where they were safe. Later that night, she came back to Dresden to rescue the others, running with them through a field full of armed men – and she was seven months pregnant at the time! It would have been really dangerous for Schumann, as a man, to be in the town; one side or other would have forced him to fight for them. Even so, one can't help feeling that sometimes Clara had a bit too much responsibility shoved onto her. Typically, Schumann's response to these violent events was to compose some gentle, idyllic music – as if he were being driven deeper into himself by the threat of the outside world.

Schumann hesitated for a long time before accepting the job in Düsseldorf; one of the reasons he didn't want to go there was that he had read that there was a mental asylum there. Maybe he had a prophetic vision?

Another prophecy...

Having not written a word for his old newspaper for nearly ten years, Schumann unexpectedly wrote an article for it a few months before he went to the asylum at Endenich. The article was about his new friend Brahms, whom Schumann praised to the skies, claiming that 'graces and heroes' had kept watch at his cradle! (That must have saved on babysitting fees, anyway.) Brahms was pleased, but embarrassed; most of his rival composers were jealous and scornful. However people reacted to it, though, the article certainly made Brahms famous. It was almost as if Schumann knew that he himself was going to be leaving the musical world, and wanted to welcome Brahms in to take his place.

Less than a year before his final collapse, Schumann became quite obsessed by a table that he insisted had magical powers. Schumann claimed that, when asked, it could tap out the rhythm of the famous opening of Beethoven's fifth symphony, and that if Schumann thought of a number, the table could guess it. Strange...

But not quite as strange...

...as something that happened about eighty years after Schumann' s death. One of Schumann's last works was his violin concerto, written for Joachim. Clara decided, after his death, that it was a weak piece, and shouldn't be published. (She took against a lot of his last works – including five Romances for cello and piano, which are now lost because she burnt the only surviving copy. Grrrrrrrrrrrrr.)

So she put the manuscript of the violin concerto into a library in Berlin, with strict instructions that it should not be touched until at least a hundred years after Schumann' s death (i.e. 1956). In the early 1930s, however, a famous Hungarian violinist, a great-niece of Joachim's, was taking part in a 'seance', a peculiar sort of event in which people claimed to be spelling out communications from the spirits of dead people. Suddenly a message appeared, telling the violinist to try to find an unpublished violin concerto composed by the spirit who was talking. "What is your name?" asked the violinist nervously. "Robert Schumann," came the answer. After this, partly because of this seance, the Schumann violin concerto was found in the Berlin library, and started to be played again. It's all most odd, and I really don't know how much truth there is in the supernatural bit – maybe a few

people already knew about the concerto, and somehow managed to play a trick on the violinist; but she at least seems really to have believed that she'd been contacted by the spirit of Schumann – and besides, it's a good story!

◆ 7 ◆

Clara survived Schumann by forty years, and played concerts (largely consisting of Schumann's music – the early works, anyway) until she was very old. She never remarried, though; and at her concerts, she always wore black.

And the children...

After Schumann left home, the children lost not only a father, but also a mother, as Clara started to travel almost constantly. Soon, they were split up from each other, too; it was a hard life. Sadly, the boys all died rather young: the oldest, Ludwig, ended up in a mental asylum, abandoned as his father had been – and for far longer. Two of the three sisters reached a good old age, though – so there's some cheerfulness in this story! Sorry for all the gloom and doom; the next chapter will be a bit merrier – honest...

Johannes Brahms

1833-1897

Baby-faced? Smooth-cheeked? A sensitive plant? Hmm...
not exactly. Brahms at fifty was unbelievably different
from Brahms at twenty – at least on the outside. Let's try
following him down the same street in Vienna (that's
where Brahms lived for the last thirty years of his life) where we
found Beethoven a couple of chapters ago. There goes Brahms,
stomping along – stomp, stomp, stomp. All around him, people
look at him, because he's famous and they recognise him – and
avert their eyes quickly, because he's fierce and doesn't like being
stared at. We'll have to hurry to keep up with him, because he walks
fast. On the other hand, there'll be some time when he gets to his
front door, because now he's got to pull his keys out of his coat
pocket and, athletic though he is, he's also more than a touch tubby
(to put it mildly); and it's probably quite difficult for him to get his
short, stubby arms across his stomach and into his coat-pocket.
Now he goes in, through his bedroom, and stomps into his study,

where he does all his composing. And now he's turning round and looking at us, his piercing blue eyes brimming with suspicion (not surprising really, since we just followed him into his apartment without an invitation). It's not just his eyes that we'd notice, though. There's something else much more startling on his face: a *beard*. Quite a beard. A thick, grey beard which landed on his face when he was forty-five. A beard so impressive – at least in the company of the rest of his head – that his picture was used in a children's geography book to show what a North German man should (or could) look like. A beard so face-changing that, when he'd just grown it, he spent a whole evening talking to a friend without the friend recognising him. A beard, in fact, so immensely bushy that you could have hidden a whole family of hamsters in it without anybody knowing (except Brahms and the hamsters, of course).

I'll bet it was prickly, too – because Brahms was by now a thoroughly prickly character (at times, anyway). (Not surprising that his favourite restaurant was called 'The Red Hedgehog'.) He'd probably ask us quite gruffly what we wanted – in a most odd voice, hoarse from all the shouting and straining he'd inflicted on it when he was young, to try to make it lower. This could be a tricky encounter. Brahms didn't really like having visitors, and would often hide in his back room and pretend he was out when people came to call. So he wouldn't appreciate you and me following him in. After a few dodgy moments, though, he might soften towards you; Brahms loved children, and was usually followed by a crowd of them on the streets – mostly because he was in the habit of giving out treats. Sometimes he'd hold candies up in the air, and give prizes to whoever jumped highest for them; sometimes he'd buy sweets that looked just like pebbles, and would then suddenly shove them into his young friends' mouths, to their initial horror, and then surprised delight. So you'd probably be OK. With grown-ups, though, he was different. If someone was in trouble, or being genuinely helpful, or Brahms just took to him or her, he could be kind, considerate, charming – a wonderful friend, in fact. But if he suspected that anybody was putting on airs, or pretending to know about things that they didn't really understand, or simply making rich people's small talk – then woe betide them! If some posh, well-dressed society woman went up to him and started simpering away about how much she'd enjoyed his music, he was liable to ask her, with heavy sarcasm, where exactly she had enjoyed it: under her blue shawl, underneath the bird on her hat, or somewhere else? The woman would retreat, blushing in shame and humiliation. He hated genteel dinner-parties, and, if he agreed to go at all, would often behave very badly. A story (made up – but true in spirit!) went around Vienna that he attended a polite gathering given by a high-class lady, and behaved so appallingly that the company couldn't wait to get rid of him; then, as he left, and his unfortunate hostess bowed him out, Brahms growled at her, "If there's anyone here this evening whom I have not offended, please offer them my apologies!"

Luckily, not even my best friends – or my worst enemies – could describe me as a polite, high-class society lady, so I *might* be spared his thunder. If I could talk really sincerely about how much his music moved me, and if he believed that I meant every word I said, he might even flush with pleasure. If he *really* liked me, he'd offer me one of his best-quality cigars; if he *quite* liked me, he'd offer me one of his second-best ones. (It wouldn't really matter, because I'd refuse either – yuk.) He might also offer to make coffee for us in his own coffee machine, of which he was mighty proud. It would be pure, strong coffee, with fresh (not boiled) cream. Once, he was in a restaurant where he was served coffee blended with chicory, a

root that costs less than coffee beans and, when boiled with water, makes good fake coffee. Brahms called over the lady who owned the restaurant. "Tell me", he purred, "do you have any chicory, by any chance?" The lady said that she did. "Amazing!" said Brahms. "Could I see it?" The owner fetched two bags of chicory for him. "Is that all you have?" Brahms inquired sadly. The lady regretted that she didn't have any more. "Good," said Brahms happily, putting both bags in his pocket. "Now, please go and make us some proper coffee!"

I might *truly* hit the bullseye with Brahms, though, if I said that I was poor (because I'd spent all my time writing a book about composers, for instance, instead of playing concerts and earning money). He'd probably offer to give me all the money I needed – so long as I didn't tell anyone about it. He was the first composer to get rich just from the sale of his music, without having to accept any commissions; and he never quite knew what to do with all his money. He sent a lot of it either to Clara Schumann or to his publisher, so that they could invest it for him; but he also gave huge amounts away – to his family, to young musicians, to musical organisations or charities, or to anyone in genuine need. One of the strangest things about Brahms was that he didn't want people to know how kind, warm and generous he could be. He really *was* a bit like a hedgehog – prickles on the outside, a soft being hidden inside. He could be horrible to young composers, telling them that they didn't know what they were doing, that they hadn't a hope of making it as a composer; but then he'd offer to support them financially so that they wouldn't have to get a job, and could spend all their time studying composition.

Sometimes he went much too far in the prickles department: once, he went to visit a family for Christmas, and just to be silly, told the children that Father Christmas (or their equivalent) had flu and couldn't bring any presents that year. The children burst out crying, and, wouldn't believe Brahms when he assured them that he'd been joking. He panicked totally, and ran to their mother to beg for her help in calming down her brood. At least that incident was quickly forgotten – but another wasn't: he gave one sensitive young composer such a hard time about his music that the poor man went completely mad, and rode around Vienna in street-cars, yelling at people to get off because Brahms had filled the carriage with dynamite. He was taken to a mental hospital, and never recovered. (Terrible – I'm sure that even Brahms, never good at apologising, must have felt dreadful about that; he was probably just trying to be helpful – but he forgot that some people are allergic to hedgehog quills.) Another time, a composer played Brahms his latest work, hoping for some praise, or at least some constructive criticism; at the end of the piece there was silence, until Brahms got up, picked up the music, and made his only comment, "What lovely manuscript paper!" Underneath all his sarcasm, though, he didn't mean to be cruel: it was just that composing was to him a sacred task, and he couldn't bear to hear bad music. And if he *did* like someone's music, he'd do a lot for them – arranging for their pieces to be published and performed for instance. He was extremely self-critical, too; he worked and worked at every piece, and was hardly ever happy with his efforts when he finished. He published only three string quartets, having written at least twenty; he burnt all the unpublished ones – as well as more than half of all the other works he wrote. He couldn't understand how Mozart could have sat down in a restaurant, or in a noisy room, and poured out great music, while he had to struggle with every note. It seemed so unfair!

I'm sure that he must have been jealous of Mozart's happy marriage, too. Brahms never married; he got close several times, but always wriggled out at the last moment, or sooner. (Do hedgehogs wriggle?) He could probably have married

Clara Schumann after Schumann had died, but he didn't; perhaps the shadow of Schumann's illness and death was too strong, and too dark. Then he fell in love with a lovely young girl called Agathe, and even gave her an engagement ring; but this was at a time when he wasn't being very successful as a composer, and he decided that he didn't want to come home after a failure, and see pity on his wife's face – so he broke off the engagement! Most odd – but that was Brahms. Another time, he decided to propose marriage to a girl on Christmas Day, and went to her house – only to be told that she'd accepted someone else's proposal a couple of hours earlier. Later, he fell in love with the Schumanns' daughter Julie (I bet Clara wasn't exactly thrilled); he was devastated when Julie married an Italian nobleman. And so on – his love-life was not exactly a success, in fact; but I think that the main reason for this was that Brahms was terrified of anybody coming too close to his inner self – he didn't want anybody finding their way past the prickles!

Even his friendships were often pretty rocky. He remained close to Clara Schumann until she died – telling her one Christmas that he loved her far more than he loved anyone else, far more than he loved himself; but they had terrible dogfights, sometimes carrying on bickering about the same little disagreement for years on end. Eventually, though, they'd always kiss and make up (without the kissing bit). But with a lot of his other friends, Brahms had quarrels – about music, about politics, about their personal lives – that would ruin the friendships. If he thought something, he'd say it – why not? Fair enough – except that sometimes it would leave people devastated. Being a friend to Brahms was no easy task; but there were rewards. If he was in a good mood, he could be warm, witty, lovable; and if his heart went out to a friend in sad times, he would do anything for them. Despite all the prickles, the growls, the sulks, he had a big heart, and could be deeply affectionate; the pity was that he didn't have a wife or children of his own on whom to lavish his affections.

So was Brahms a miserable, sad man, who gave up his whole life for music? I think not. Despite all his moaning and groaning about being lonely, he always had company, whether in Vienna or in the country towns where he spent his summers. He had fine old times sitting in outdoor restaurants, listening to gypsies play blazing melodies on their violins, or to dance-orchestras playing graceful Viennese waltzes. Or he might sit indoors at a beer-hall – consuming a huge amount of beer, which did his figure no good at all – and telling a group of admiring young musicians all about what was what in life, and hearing them laugh uproariously at all his jokes. It's true that, at the end of the evening, he'd trundle home all alone – but at least when he got there, he could know that his works were loved and appreciated all over the musical world. And perhaps it was just as well that when he went to sleep, he did so without a wife next to him – because his snoring would have driven her to madness, and then he'd really have had something to moan and groan about...

The Music

As I said, Brahms used to work and work at everything he wrote, and destroyed most of what he composed. An idea would occur to him; he'd think about it for ages while he took long walks through the countryside (like Beethoven), and only when he'd considered it from every possible angle would he finally write it down. It was then that the struggle would *really* begin, while he laboured to improve on what he had written. Eventually, he would send the completed piece to a friend whose judgment he trusted, with a note saying what a bad piece it was. If they made suggestions, he'd sometimes take their advice, sometimes ignore it; whichever, he was bound to work on the piece some more. Then he'd make sure that the piece was at least tried through, and preferably performed, before finally, finally, sending it off to be published – again, usually with a note saying that it wasn't worth publishing.

So one could say, without being worried about being 100 percent wrong, that writing music didn't exactly come easily to Hedgehog Brahms. He adored the music of the great masters of the past – Bach, Mozart, Beethoven and others; and most of his works are in the 'forms' of earlier times: symphonies, sonatas, concertos, quartets, etc. (but no opera – Brahms never wrote one). He was sure that those geniuses of the past had had all the best ideas, and that he could never match them; but he still wanted to model his works on theirs – what better way to learn? (Of course, although he didn't think much of his own music, he thought even less of the music of most of the other composers of his time!) And so his music is a continuation of the ideals of his predecessors. Some of Brahms' contemporaries, who were busily trying to sweep away the forms of the past and create their own new ones, thought that Brahms was an old fogey, just trying to rewrite old music. Wrong! Brahms' great achievement was to take old forms and transform them into living, breathing, fresh creations.

He wrote music in all sorts of moods: sometimes one can hear him relaxing, enjoying himself, a glass of beer in his hand, perhaps listening to a gypsy orchestra. (He wrote twenty-one 'Hungarian Dances', based on gypsy melodies; and one can often hear the wild gypsy spirit in his larger works, too). At other times, one can feel clearly the darker, tragic side of his nature. In some of his fast movements, the ones called 'scherzo' (pronounced 'skertso,' originally meaning 'joke' – some joke!), one can almost hear demons chasing through dark forests – scary. Then there are thrashing seas, glorious sunsets, love-songs, graceful dances – and so on. What binds them together, marks them out as the work of the same composer, is a richness, a deep and magnificent beauty (usually distinctly unprickly, by the way) that is Brahms' musical voice – and no-one else's! If I switch on the radio without knowing what's going to be on, it's so easy to know if it's Brahms that's being played; it comes sweeping out, dragging me along, refusing to let me switch off again – very inconvenient if I'm in a hurry! But it's worth spending the time to listen...

What to listen to

Since Brahms tore up anything he didn't like, there are no really bad, or even unimportant, works by him around today. (Many of the 'Hungarian Dances', and other shorter works, are light and fun, but not unimportant – it's important to have fun!) Perhaps the very greatest Brahms works, though, were those written when he was feeling something very deeply in his life, but (being the human hedgehog he was) was only able to express those feelings through music. The first piano concerto, for instance, was written after Schumann's death – and a lot of it sounds like the cry of a soul in torment. I remember the first time I heard it: I jumped several inches at the opening crash from the timpani (drum). The first movement is really anguished; it's only in the slow, prayer-like second movement that one can feel the spirit of Schumann being laid to rest. Try the violin concerto, too – a very different animal; it's got some of the most beautiful melodies that he ever wrote, and a rollicking last movement, full of gypsy-style rhythms. His 'German Requiem' is absolutely gorgeous – a gentle, touching lament written after the death of his mother. Then there are the symphonies: Brahms had been planning to write a symphony for at least twenty years before he dared produce his first one – but it was worth waiting for. It's got a magnificent, dark opening – also with pounding timpani – that seems to announce the birth of an exciting new world. Perhaps the most famous symphony is the last, no. 4: it starts with a glorious melody that you might like to listen to first thing in the morning. It could even make getting up a bit easier! Another of my favourite pieces is the clarinet quintet, op. 115; it's one of his last works, and one can almost hear the coals glowing in a dying fire, with wise old gypsies sitting around telling their wild, sad tales. These are all pretty long pieces, though; if you want to hear a short gem by Brahms, try his famous 'Lullaby'. You may well find that you know it; it crops up everywhere – in arrangements for all sorts of instruments, on music-boxes, on annoyingly loud mobile-phone rings, etc. – that's not Brahms' fault! At least it's a tune worth remembering – and if a tune has to get stuck in your head, it might as well be a good one. Anyway, it's hard to go wrong with his music: as I said, there's no really weak piece. Try listening to as many of his works as you like, long or short – and just let yourself fall in love with them!

Facts of Life

①

Brahms was born in 1833 in the North German city of Hamburg; he was a real Hamburger, in fact! His parents were an odd couple, unlikely parents for a great artist; neither of them was particularly well educated, for a start. It's hard to know where Brahms got his ambition and his thirst for learning; he was really a self-made genius. Brahms' mother, Christiane, was a cautious, shy woman, seventeen years older than his father, Johann Jakob. *He* was outgoing and flirtatious, and probably a bit of a rogue. Christiane was forty-one when they married, but still managed to produce three children – Johannes, Elise and Fritz; that's pretty impressive! Johann Jakob and Christiane weren't really happy together, though. He earned a fair amount as a freelance musician, playing all sorts of different instruments; but whenever he earned anything, he'd want to spend it on yet more instruments – much to Christiane's disgust. She had to work as a seamstress in order for the family to live comfortably. Long after all the children had grown up, Johann Jakob and Christiane separated. Brahms, now thirty-one years old, was devastated and tried, unsuccessfully, to reconcile his parents.

Proud parents..?

A photo of Brahms' mother, taken three years before she died, shows a smiling old woman, obviously dressed up in her very best clothes for the photo. She is rather lacking – actually, completely lacking – in the tooth department; but one can guess from the photo that she must have had a very kind heart. She adored Brahms, and he her; but he was equally fond of his naughty father. Johann Jakob, for his part, must have been immensely proud of Johannes; but he had a strange way of showing it. After one of the great triumphs of Brahms' life, the first performance of his Requiem, someone asked Johann Jakob what he thought.

"Didn't sound bad," he replied nonchalantly, taking a pinch of snuff. What a cool dude...

Elise, Brahms' sister, was a rather fragile character. When she married, quite late in life, Brahms predicted disaster, and complained about her getting married at all since, he declared rather surprisingly, he had stayed single for Elise's sake! A bit hard to see the logic of that – to put it mildly. Anyway, her marriage turned out happily, and he was reconciled to it. He was happier, though, about his father's second marriage; Brahms adored his stepmother, and continued to support her, and her son from a previous marriage (i.e. Brahms' father's stepson – what relation does that make him to Brahms??) generously after his father's death. Brahms was always handing over money to his family – even to Fritz...

The 'wrong' brother...

Fritz and Johannes did not get along well. Fritz must be one of the most unfortunate characters in the history of music. He tried to make it as a pianist, and even became quite well-known as a teacher; but his brother's fame and fortune always put his achievements into the darkest of shades. The charming name by which he was known in Hamburg was 'the wrong Brahms' – isn't that terrible? Not surprisingly, he tried to get as far away as possible, and went off to Venezuela, in South America, to teach the piano. That didn't work out either, though, and after a couple of years he had to come home again to Hamburg. He tried to make the most of his own career there, giving concerts in which he tried to play some of his brother's most difficult piano music – without much success, it seems. Brahms got furious with him for failing to support their parents and sister, and the two brothers ended up hardly on speaking terms. Fritz may have been irresponsible, and possibly he was quite unpleasant; but who wouldn't have been, with a name like 'the wrong Brahms'? I'm surprised he didn't end up shooting people.

Brahms' early life was fairly uneventful on the surface. He studied the piano (and for a time, the cello and the horn as well) avidly, earned money by playing dance-music, started to compose, and got pretty frustrated by being stuck in Hamburg, unknown and unappreciated. Then came a chance to travel, which led to his meeting with Schumann, and Schumann's article praising him to the skies. Actually, the skies weren't very interested; but music-lovers all over Germany were. Brahms was suddenly famous – and was expected to produce great music. The pressure of all this, plus the shock-horror of Schumann's illness and death, as well as the slightly awkward fact of his being madly in love with Schumann's wife, had a violent effect on him; suddenly he found he couldn't compose any more!

Love letters...

After Schumann had been taken to the asylum at Endenich, Brahms spent most of his time at the Schumanns' house, looking after the children while Clara went on concert tours, and sorting out Schumann's wonderful music library – getting to know huge amounts of music and learning lots about composition in the process. He also wrote passionate letters to Clara. In later life, they returned their letters to each other and set about burning them. (Brahms liked fires.) Clara destroyed a lot of hers to him – including all those from the time when Brahms was in love with her (and she with him? We'll never know for sure – but I'm pretty sure that she was). Somehow, though, lots of his outpourings to her survived, even the most impassioned ones. He would have been furious if he'd known that we can read them today. In later life, he burnt as many letters to and from himself as he could, just to prevent people in the future writing about his love for various women, his prickliness to other friends, and so on – just what I'm writing about! Sorry to intrude, Mr. Hedgehog; the trouble is – you were too interesting...

◄ 4 ►

Eventually, Brahms decided that he had to earn a living – and had to get away from Clara, before he died of love for her, or married her (both terrifying prospects). So he went back to Hamburg, where he was able to compose again – at last. His music had changed, though. The pieces he had taken to Schumann had been wild, free, modern-sounding. After his terrible creative block, he found that his way back to composing lay through his studies in Schumann's library. For the future, he would rely on the past! His music became more controlled, more balanced – more like the classics of the old masters, in fact. He wouldn't fly off into strange ideas, as he had earlier; his music was still just as full of feeling, of course – but now his strange fantasies had become transformed into proper stories.

Not quite a hit...

By 1858, he was finally ready to present a big work to the public: his first piano concerto, one of his stormiest, most violent pieces. The first performance, in Hanover, went all right, and Brahms had high hopes for the second, in the important city of Leipzig. As he played it in the concert, he gradually became aware that the audience was not exactly loving it. At the end, he got up and faced the public; three people tried to clap – but were immediately drowned out by other people hissing and booing. Not QUITE the success Brahms had hoped for.

Even though he was composing again, Brahms knew he had to earn some money more quickly than he could from his compositions (especially after the Leipzig disaster). So he started giving concerts as a pianist, and teaching. He also conducted a women's chorus; he enjoyed that – a whole group of pretty young girls looking at him adoringly as he directed them. Sometimes they would rehearse outside – and once, Brahms conducted them from above, sitting in a tree! That must have been fun for everybody (except for the tree, perhaps).

Not a natural performer...

*Brahms was not a natural performer. He didn't enjoy giving
concerts: he wasn't keen on audiences, and he got very nervous.
Besides, he didn't really like practising the piano, and needed to be
bullied into it; if he was visiting the Schumann family, the eldest
daughter, Marie, would sternly send him off to practise his scales
straight after breakfast. In later life, Brahms got noisier and
noisier as he played, grunting and groaning for all he was worth.
A friend was once standing outside the room where Brahms was
composing at the piano; from all the howling and whining
accompanying the music, the friend was surprised to realise that
Brahms must have acquired a dog. Eventually, the door was
opened, and out came – no dog, but just an embarrassed-looking
Brahms, very cross to have been overheard in his canine effusions.
(Brahms never owned a dog, by the way; but he did have at least
one dog-friend, a Scottish terrier named Argos. Argos belonged to
a Swiss companion of Brahms, who lost the poor little dog on the
top of a mountain in bad weather. The man returned home, alone
and miserable. Three days later, while Brahms was visiting his
friend, and probably trying to cheer him up, there was a scratch at*

the door – and there, leaping triumphantly, was Argos, having somehow found his way home! Brahms and his friend were thrilled.)

Although he kept rooms in Hamburg, Brahms started to travel more and more – especially after the Hamburg Philharmonic Orchestra refused to appoint him as their chief conductor. He went around Germany and Switzerland, playing and conducting his own works and other music. Eventually, though, he had to settle somewhere, and in 1869 he chose Vienna, home to so many great composers of the past. He even accepted an appointment as conductor of one of the major musical societies, introducing the public to a lot of forgotten old masterpieces; but he gave it up after three years – Brahms couldn't be tied to anything or anybody. He stayed in Vienna for the rest of his life, however, living in a modest rented apartment, with a nice view of the Karlskirche, a famous old church, just outside his window. The lively city, with its busy musical life and its exciting mixture of different nationalities, suited Brahms down to the Viennese ground.

Although his home was now Vienna...

*...Brahms would spend his summers in country places in
Germany, Austria or Switzerland. (He also went on several
holidays to Italy, which he loved; but generally he
avoided non-German-speaking countries.
He was hopeless at foreign
languages!) It was during these
summers that he got most of his
composing done, tramping
through the countryside, going
through his new pieces in his
head. He'd always make sure that
he had friends in attendance, though,
for when he wanted company; he'd
command them to join him wherever he
was – and one didn't refuse Brahms! Sometimes he'd even drag
them along on mountain-climbing expeditions – rather an
unlikely occupation for someone with Brahms' figure (in later life,
anyway). He'd usually puff and mutter away about how stupid he
was to be doing this as they climbed upwards – but coming down
would put him in a far better mood, as he drew closer and closer
to good food and drink...*

As Brahms grew older, he felt that his music was becoming old-
fashioned, and that younger, 'fashionable' composers were on
the wrong path and were ruining the future of music. Many of
them were being influenced by Brahms' great rival, Richard
Wagner – pronounced 'Vahgner' – who wrote huge operas based
on old German legends. He was a thoroughly unsavoury
character, but a great composer – and his ideas were impossible
to ignore. There were a few composers whom Brahms loved –
notably Johann Strauss, the 'Waltz-King', who wrote the famous
'Blue Danube' waltz, among piles of other charming music;

and Dvorak, a wonderful, almost child-like Czech composer who was made really famous by Brahms. (Brahms even went through Dvorak's new works, making sure there weren't any mistakes before they were sent off to the printer, when Dvorak was away and couldn't do it for himself – a lovely thing for one composer to do for another.) As for himself, Brahms believed that by 1890, at the age of fifty-seven, he had written his last work, and it was time to retire. Luckily, inspiration returned, and he couldn't resist it. Part of it came from hearing a wonderful clarinettist, for whom Brahms wrote four great works. There are also some amazing late piano pieces – exploring new worlds – and his last major work, 'Four Serious Songs', all concerned with the theme of death. Not exactly a laugh a minute – but wise and beautiful music.

Brahms on record...

Even if he was an old fogey in many ways, Brahms was fascinated by some new inventions – the electric light and photography, for instance. (He disapproved of bicycles, though – too fast and too noisy, according to Brahms!) One new invention he tried out was a primitive recording machine invented by the great Thomas Edison. There is a wax cylinder (a very old sort of disc) in existence on which somebody mutters something – and then suddenly a high voice leaps out at us, saying, "I am Doctor Brahms! Johannes Brahms!" (At least, that's what it sounds like – it's a bit hard to be sure exactly what is said – or who's saying it.) Then there's a lot of scratch and hiss, and a rather out-of-tune sounding piano, just

audible from time to time. Apparently, this is Brahms playing his own Hungarian Dance No. 1. It's frustrating, but fascinating.

The death of Clara Schumann in 1896 was a heavy blow to Brahms. To lose his closest friend was terrible; he must have known that he himself would follow before too long. To make matters worse, in his hurry to get to her funeral, he took two wrong trains, and took more than forty hours to get there, finally arriving, exhausted and desperate, after the funeral had begun.

A friendship revived...

His other oldest friend, Joseph Joachim, who had introduced him to the Schumanns, survived him; but the friendship had weakened many years earlier. Brahms had always been annoyed by Joachim's constant worry over whether Brahms really, really liked him; hedgehogs don't like being asked those sorts of questions! The real break came, though, when Joachim tried to get divorced, Mrs. Joachim contested it, and Brahms took her side. The two men didn't speak for years; but Joachim continued to play Brahms' music. Eventually, Brahms broke the silence by writing a 'double concerto' for violin, cello and orchestra. It has several little messages to Joachim in it – a quote from one of Joachim's favourite pieces; several uses of Joachim's musical motto 'F.A.E.', (which stands for 'Frei Aber Einsam' – 'Free but Lonely'); and a series of quarrels between the violin and the cello that end up all (musical) smiles. Joachim couldn't resist, and the two of them resumed their friendship, although on a rather more distant basis than before. Joachim may have been a bit of a pain at times, but so was Brahms! When one of Joachim's sons was born, Brahms wrote him a letter of 'congratulations', moaning that it was now too late to wish the little boy the best of all fates – never to have been born at all. A charming way of spreading light and cheer...

Shortly after Clara's death, Brahms started to look ill himself; his skin turned yellow, and later almost green. He started to lose weight, although he denied it, pointing out that his clothes still fitted him. In fact, his landlady used to steal in when he was asleep, and secretly let in the clothes, so that Brahms wouldn't know how thin he was becoming. Soon, it became obvious that he was dying (even though he made light of the illness himself). The Viennese audience gave him a wonderful farewell ovation at a performance of the fourth symphony; Brahms stood acknowledging the applause with tears streaming down his cheeks. His spikes were softening; he actually started being unashamedly nice to people! He died on April 3rd, 1897. His last words had been to a friend who handed him a glass of white wine, "Ah – that tasted fine! You're a kind man." It was a surprisingly gentle way for a prickly hedgehog to go – but by then the real Brahms was showing through.

A fond farewell...

Vienna gave him a splendid funeral, full of pomp, ceremony, music and speeches. Brahms might have had a dry word or two to say about it all! In his rooms were found a set of chorale preludes for organ, the last music he'd worked on. The last of the set is called 'O Welt, ich mus dich lassen' ('O World, I must leave you'). Like Bach before him, Brahms left us a religious chorale as a farewell – as if to tell us that he was prepared for his end. Naturally, it was with music that he chose to say goodbye.

Igor Stravinsky

1882-1971

All right, I'll admit it: I'm not too keen on boiled eggs. Actually, I like the taste, but I'm not sure they're really worth all the trouble. For a start, I usually make a mess of breaking open the shell, and I get nasty gritty bits mixed up in the white. Then (with soft-boiled eggs) I like to dunk my toast soldiers; but when I do, the yolk spills out and runs down the side, and I have to mop it up before it congeals. Yuk. Still, I'm always pleased when I see a boiled egg waiting unbroken at the breakfast-table – mostly because it reminds me of Igor Stravinsky's head. It's funny, really, because Stravinsky was never *completely* bald; and eggs don't, as a rule, have huge ears, an enormous nose, glasses (especially glasses perched on the top of their heads) or a moustache – but there's definitely a resemblance. Maybe it's because Stravinsky was both an egghead (i.e. thoroughly clever) and in some ways a hard-boiled character, who quite deserved to be tapped on the head with a teaspoon from time to time.

Underneath his egghead, though, Stravinsky's body looked more like a stick-insect than an egg cup. He was tiny, and so thin that there was almost nothing to him. I once saw a revolting horror film about a little baby monster who was swaddled in a huge bandage; eventually, his father, who was human – sort-of – wanted to see what was underneath the bandage, so he unwrapped it. He discovered too late that the bandage *was* the monster's body – and he'd just taken it off! Quite disgusting – but it does remind me a bit of Stravinsky, somehow, especially since Stravinsky, who was terrified of catching colds, tended to go around with his tiny body swaddled in scarves, sweaters, coats and a beret (which he sometimes wore in bed!).

He didn't just look like an insect, he also behaved a lot like one in many ways; a very neat and orderly one – perhaps an ant rather than a stick-insect? Everything he owned – and he hoarded lots of stuff – had to be sorted into tidy piles; untidiness, or clumsiness (or people with loud voices) horrified him. Wherever he went – and he lived in lots of different places at various times in his life, as well as travelling around the world conducting orchestras and playing the piano – he insisted on order around him. His favourite place would always be his studio, which had to be soundproofed, so that he could compose at the piano (which would be muted, so that it made hardly any noise) without being overheard by anybody. He would surround himself there with his treasures – gifts, souvenirs, photos and so on. The piano would be covered with stuff, too: on its music-stand, a board on which would be clipped his sketches for the piece he was writing; and on the side his writing-tools, gleaming like doctors' surgical instruments – steel pens, pencils, erasers, sharpeners, metronomes, stopwatches. Everything in its place, everything under control – that's how Stravinsky liked it.

Insect egghead or not, he was very vain about his appearance. He would spend ages in front of mirrors; and if he had a pimple on his nose, he'd probably cancel plans to go out. He'd also refuse to go anywhere – or alternatively, he'd refuse to stay in a room – if he suspected that he might come in contact with germs. If somebody sneezed or coughed, there was liable to be a Stravinsky-shaped hole where the egghead had just been. Actually, that rather extreme reaction wasn't unusual for Stravinsky; he reacted strongly to *everything*. He was curious about all sorts of things – and furious about all sorts of things. It didn't take much to make Stravinsky angry: the slightest criticism of his music would do it. So would any performer who ignored any of Stravinsky's instructions in his music (or, for that matter, any performer who earned more from performing a piece than Stravinsky had from composing it). Taxes would make him hopping mad, too. Stravinsky loved and adored money – and the thought of someone taking it away from him was enough to make him foam at the ears. He would save money in any way he could think of. For instance, if Stravinsky noticed that a letter had arrived with a stamp on it that hadn't been marked by the post office, he'd make sure to remove and reuse it. (He damaged several letters from famous people in this way – letters that would have been hundreds of times more valuable than the stamps!) He'd spend precious time copying out music himself rather than paying to have it copied; and he'd rack his brains to think of a way to write a telegram conveying as much information as he could in as few words as possible, since extra words cost extra money. When anybody invited him to compose a new piece, or to give a concert, Stravinsky would move into action, waving his insect-legs in the air (metaphorically speaking, I hasten to add) to attract as much money as possible. Hmm... he *loved* the stuff. (To be fair, there were times when he desperately needed it, particularly during and just after World War One, when he was cut off from possessions in his native Russia, and had not only his first wife Catherine and their four children to feed, but also Catherine's sister and her family – a lot of mouths and stomachs!)

Talking of wives: Stravinsky's second wife, Vera, was another of the great loves of his life. She was charming, beautiful, vivacious and a talented painter – and she could cope with Stravinsky and his rages! She was quite a contrast from the serious, devoutly religious Catherine, who was probably scared stiff of her husband. Whereas Catherine would write him letters timidly chiding him for neglecting his religious duties, Vera would write to him demanding the latest gossip: 'tell me who was amusing, and who was stupid'. I'm sure that Stravinsky must have loved Catherine and the children too – but he had a strange way of showing it. Catherine was his first cousin, and Stravinsky had grown up with her; they were married when they were both very young, well before Stravinsky became famous. After he became successful, and while he was still married to Catherine, Stravinsky had several fairly public love-affairs, the most serious of which was with Vera (who was also married when they fell in love). Since Stravinsky was basically a very religious man, a Russian Orthodox Christian who firmly believed in both God and the Devil (and was constantly crossing himself), he probably felt very guilty; but he went ahead with the affairs anyway. Poor Catherine was very ill for much of her life, and spent long periods in a sanatorium; Stravinsky would often be travelling on concert tours, or for meetings, and would frequently take Vera with him. Catherine sometimes had to rely on Vera for news of her own husband! Also, Catherine was sometimes left with hardly enough money to live on while Stravinsky was off cavorting in luxury with Vera. Catherine would have to write begging letters to them both, asking for money to be sent home! It was a strange situation, to say the least – the strangest thing of all being that both women seem to have put up with it fairly uncomplainingly, and even to have been (on the surface, at least) friends. Most odd; but Stravinsky did have an extraordinary way of making everybody around him do exactly what he wanted them to do. He was quite open about using people. When the conductor who made a lot of Stravinsky's earlier works famous, Ansermet ('Anserm-A') wrote to him at the end of 1929 congratulating him on a very productive twelve months, Stravinsky wrote back, agreeing wholeheartedly that he'd been writing wonderful music that year, and added: 'What should I wish for you [i.e. for the New Year], egotist that I am, but the continuation of your superb activity in the publicising of my music?' Hmm... others might have wished him health, happiness, success in everything he did, etc. – but not Stravinsky. Oh well – at least he *knew* that he was an egotist.

Another of Stravinsky's passions was for alcohol – especially whisky. He would drink it all day every day, given half the chance; as he himself said: "My name should be Strawhisky!" When he was very old, it would sometimes do him more good than any medicines; but there were a lot of times when it *didn't* do him much good. For instance, there was an occasion on which he was supposed to meet with a great painter called Marc Chagall, to discuss a possible collaboration. Unfortunately, Stravinsky went out for lunch before the meeting, and drank so much that when the time came to meet Chagall, he was fast asleep and nobody could wake him up. Funnily enough, the collaboration didn't happen! Another time, Stravinsky was awarded a huge honour by the government of the USA – a dinner for him at the White House, hosted by the then-President of America, John F. Kennedy. Stravinsky got extremely drunk, had to be helped to the men's loo by the President, and was taken home early, in dire disgrace – in Vera's books, at least. She was relieved, though, that her husband hadn't managed to get the President of the USA into a corner and ask him how to avoid paying tax, as he'd planned to do – Stravinsky could be *so* embarrassing! (Incidentally, when J.F.K. was assassinated not long afterwards, Stravinsky sent a telegram of condolence to his widow – but wanted to send it overnight, to take advantage of cheap night rates. Again, Vera was not impressed.)

Yet another of Stravinsky's obsessions was with his own health – despite his love of alcohol, of rich foods and of smoking. (Hmm... I've noticed that all of the composers in this book loved alcohol, tobacco and coffee; no wonder they're all dead!) He used to keep detailed medical diaries, reporting all the medication that he was constantly taking, and all of his symptoms. Being Stravinsky, he expected everybody around him to be as concerned with his health as he was; even when Catherine was dying, he would write her long letters complaining about all *his* health problems. It's true that there were times, even when he was quite young, when he was seriously ill, with tuberculosis and other illnesses; but he was also a hypochondriac. For instance, a reporter once called him unexpectedly, asking for an interview when Stravinsky didn't feel like giving one; just as an impromptu excuse, Stravinsky said that he couldn't talk, because he had a cold – and then, forgetting that he'd just made that up for convenience, he spent the rest of the day moping around, convinced that he actually *did* have a cold!

But of all his many loves, passions and obsessions, the most important of all was music, of course. When he was very old and in hospital, a nurse asked him if he wanted anything, "I want to work [i.e. compose]" replied Stravinsky, "and if I can't work, I want to die." I shouldn't think that any composer has ever taken his or her music more seriously than Stravinsky did his (despite the fact that he wrote many light, humorous pieces). He was convinced of the importance of virtually every one of his works; when asked to recommend one particular piece, his response was, "I recommend ALL my works." His whole life revolved around composing. Performing his music – first as a pianist and then, increasingly, as a conductor – was also very important to him, and took a huge amount of his time, involving travels around the world; but the main reasons he did so much of it were that it earned more money than composing (the wrong way round, I'd say, but that's how it was) and that it allowed him to present his works in the way he wanted them to be played. It was rare for him to hear one of his works performed by someone else without getting furious. (If he went to someone else's concert, he might have to listen to music by another contemporary composer, too, which he usually hated. He was pretty good at avoiding seeing or hearing music by other people. Once, an unfortunate young man was foolish enough to ask

Stravinsky to look through the new symphony that the young man had just written. Stravinsky told him to come to his hotel the next day. The composer duly arrived, symphony in hand. "Oh, I'm too busy now," said Stravinsky. "When can I show you my symphony, then?" asked the young composer. Stravinsky consulted his diary. "Tomorrow – no. Next week – no." He went on through his diary, then snapped it shut. "How about never – does that suit you?" Hmm... not the *nicest* story.)

So music (and, to a certain extent, the other arts: Stravinsky knew, and cared, a lot about painting – he was a talented artist himself – theatre, literature, dance and so on) was at the centre of his life – his *own* music, that is. Other people had to realise that and, if they were to be his friends, to make sure that Stravinsky's music was at the centre of *their* lives, too – otherwise Stravinsky wouldn't be interested in them. Hmm... yet another rather-less-than-charming characteristic. Am I giving you a bad impression of him? Well, it's true that Stravinsky wasn't always the most sympathetic of men; I do think that he was a shiny, brittle insect, with a pretty deadly sting. But on the other hand he was fascinating – incredibly lively and intelligent, his mind always buzzing with new and exciting ideas; he was often very funny, and could even be surprisingly generous at times; and – particularly as he got older, I suspect – he could be strangely and irresistibly charming.

Of the six composers in this book he is, of course, the only one that we can see on old television films, hear on many recordings, and of whom we can hear first-hand accounts from people still alive today. So it should be fairly easy to imagine what it was like to visit him in his house in Hollywood in, say, 1947 – when Stravinsky

was a sprightly sixty-four, Vera a bubbly fifty-nine. We wouldn't dare visit him, mind you, unless he and Vera had invited us first. If he didn't want us there, Stravinsky would be quite capable of answering the door himself, and telling us that he was out! But as long as they expected us, the Stravinskys would make us quite welcome in their crowded little house. If we arrived early enough, we might be greeted by the sight of Stravinsky's feet pointing upwards over the balcony; he had a whole daily routine, including

vigorous exercises, which he practised regularly, "Every morning for fifteen minutes I pray, for fifteen minutes I exercise, for fifteen minutes I shave." (That's a long time to spend shaving!) Of course, we might not see him at all, if by the time we arrived he was working in his study, with the door shut; then woe betide anyone foolish enough to open it! If we were to wander around while we waited for him to emerge from his lair, we might find a note from Vera reminding herself of all the day's tasks; at the top, Stravinsky would have scrawled 'First, you have to kiss me.' At lunchtime, Vera would go to the hallway beneath his study and clap her hands, to tell him that lunch was ready; provided that he was ready too,

Stravinsky would clap his hands in reply, and emerge. "How are you, Mr Stravinsky?" we would ask; "So-so la-la," would probably be the reply, in his richly accented Russian voice. Then we'd sit down to lunch – probably washed down by lots of alcohol. (I trust that you'd refuse that bit?!) During the meal, the conversation could stretch from a fascinating diatribe about music or the arts in general, to an unnecessarily graphic description of Stravinsky's latest activities in the bathroom – not the *perfect* mealtime topic for us guests, perhaps, but he'd assume that we were riveted. There might be long pauses if he became interested in an English word, and went off to consult a dictionary. He was fascinated by languages – he spoke four fluently, used seven in his music, and had written out a whole English dictionary for himself when he came to live in America. After lunch, we might be introduced to Popka the parrot, who would be allowed to fly around the room – and possibly settle on our heads (fine, so long as that's all he did). Popka would then probably do his party-trick, opening the cage of his friend Lyssaya Dushka (Bald Darling) the canary, so that there'd be two birds whizzing around the room. (Outside on the porch there was a cage full of lovebirds, as well.) We'd also meet Vasska the cat, a very important person indeed – and very spoiled. When the Stravinskys adopted another cat, Vasska was so upset and jealous that he made himself ill, and the Stravinskys ended up dumping the other poor cat sixteen kilometres (ten miles) away with a little note around his neck saying that he was up for adoption – terrible! (He found his way back to the Stravinsky's house, though –

clever puss.)

At some stage, Stravinsky would have to deal with his post; he received so much that he had to have a specially large mailbox made. A lot of it would be fan-mail, asking for his autograph; he would only *think* of responding if there was a stamped, self-addressed envelope enclosed. There might also be a letter from somebody he'd known in the dim and distant past; he was quite likely to ignore these letters – Stravinsky lived in the present. Then he might be sent newspaper articles or letters talking about his music; with these, he would make (usually angry) underlined comments in the margins. And finally, there would be business letters about forthcoming concerts – to which he'd generally reply with a demand for more money, more rehearsal-time, etc.

That out of the way, and if he'd decided to forgo work for the rest of the day, he'd probably have a glass of weak tea with bread and cakes with jam, and a game of solitaire – two if he lost the first one. After that, he might take us shopping. He was very serious about his shopping, and loved walking up and down the aisles of supermarkets, admiring the neatly stacked shelves; but before he bought anything, there'd be a suspicious enquiry, "How much is it costing?". Or, if we were unlucky, he'd drag us off to the cinema, where he'd give a loud running commentary on the film and annoy everybody. Then he would (if he was feeling *really* friendly) take us out to a swanky restaurant, where he'd order the best food and drink, boss the waiters around, and provide sparkling conversation (but also stopping occasionally to draw pictures on the tablecloth of any woman in the restaurant whose shape caught his fancy).

Stravinsky might give us vivid descriptions of his dreams; he would remember them clearly, and claimed to solve most of his musical problems while asleep. He'd probably start an argument, or start saying rude things about another composer's music – "Who needs it?" (his favourite expression of disgust). If he was in a good mood, though – and Vera would try to steer him onto topics that kept him sunny ("He is very nice when he thinks not about music," was her opinion) – he would be great fun, and we'd party until late into the night, probably until Stravinsky announced, "I am dronk!" Then it'd be back to their place and if you were staying the night, no bed but a couch (the Stravinskys would have asked for your measurements by letter before you arrived, just to make sure you fitted their famous couch); and lights out before too long, or Stravinsky might reappear and scold you for not being asleep – he'd do that to anybody. So probably best to try and get some sleep before another day with this perpetually active insect egghead...

The Music

In a way, it's more difficult to describe Stravinsky's music than to describe the music of the other composers in this book. With them, although their style of composing developed hugely during their lives, their basic musical language remained the same, just becoming more individual and unique. With Stravinsky, his whole style and language changed completely, several times over; the personality remains clearly Stravinsky, but it is like a writer who, having written his first books in Russian, changes to French, then English, then German. Many of Stravinsky's earlier works are influenced by folk tales and customs from his native Russia – lots of magic, primitive rituals (Stravinsky loved rituals) and exotic dances. Then, as he started to feel more cut off from Russia, he took music from the eighteenth century as his model, so that some of his pieces sound half like old music and half like Stravinsky. (As he said, "The past is a nest in which I feel comfortable laying my eggs.") Finally, when he came back to Europe for a visit after World War Two, he started to feel that his music was old-fashioned by comparison with what was being written there. After that he began to write much more 'modern' music – full of dissonances, where notes fight against each other instead of combining to make beautiful chords.

Stravinsky's views on what music *means* were very different from those of the other composers in this book, too. Where Schumann, for instance, felt that everything that happened in his life immediately found its way into his music, Stravinsky felt that his life had nothing to do with his music. "Music is just music," he said. It wasn't that he thought that it doesn't express anything; he just felt that music expresses its own emotions, not our everyday human feelings. Even when he set words to music, he was often more interested in the *sounds* of the words than in their meanings.

Stravinsky was interested in all sounds, new and old. He loved the elegant music of the eighteenth century; he was also very interested in jazz, and wrote ragtimes and polkas. If he found a folk instrument he didn't know, he'd be fascinated; and he was always trying out new combinations of orchestral instruments. (He had an amazing ear: he could hear seven distinct pitches in the noise of a plane flying overhead.) This is partly what makes getting to know his music such an adventure: he's always trying out something new and unexpected. I have to say that some of his pieces do sound to me like experiments, rather than great music. (Maybe I just don't know them well enough, or can't understand them; but that's the way I feel – how furious Stravinsky would have been to read that! No doubt he'd have written in red, heavily underlined, in the margin: 'So, if he doesn't understand it, why does he write about it?' Sorry, Mr. S – I'm just expressing my opinion. "Who needs it?") But as for the major masterpieces: well, he may have said that his music wasn't expressing human emotions, but he certainly never said that we shouldn't feel human emotions when we listen to it! The colours, the rhythms, the unearthly sounds; he can make you laugh, he can make you cry, he can make you dance – in fact, he can send you a bit crazy! And it's a wonderful feeling...

What to listen to

I'd recommend starting with the three great ballet-scores which made Stravinsky famous: 'The Firebird', 'Petrushka' and 'The Rite of Spring'. 'The Firebird' is full of wonderful bright colours and vivid characters; 'Petrushka', about a puppet who comes to life in a market place, bustles with life, magic and humour. But the greatest of all, I think, is 'The Rite of Spring'.
When this was first played in Paris in 1913 (as a ballet, although it really doesn't need dancers at all – the music by itself is quite enough for anyone to cope with), a riot erupted! People jeered and cheered, booed and bravoed, shouted and screamed; fights broke out and the police had to be called in. (A year later, the music was performed again at a concert in Paris, and provoked another riot – but this one was 100 percent enthusiasm; Stravinsky was hoisted onto the shoulders of a huge crowd and carried around the streets of Paris in triumph.) It's not surprising that 'The Rite' drove people mad: inspired by an ancient Russian ceremony welcoming the arrival of spring, it is filled with weird, hypnotic sounds, violent stomping rhythms and primitive passion. Listen to it – it's an amazing experience. (Disney uses some of 'The Rite of Spring' to accompany dinosaurs fighting in the old film *Fantasia*; Stravinsky was scornful about this, of course – but I think Disney had a point.

There's a lot of other wonderful music, too: 'Les Noces', written for chorus, percussion and four pianos, depicts, in a strange but fascinating way, another ancient Russian ceremony – this time a peasant wedding. 'A Symphony of Psalms', a full-voiced, full-hearted song of praise is dedicated 'to the glory of God'; or try 'Renard', a music-theatre piece based on a Russian folk-tale about a wicked fox. There are some fun shorter pieces, as well, such as 'Ragtime' for eleven instruments, and 'Circus Polka', written for fifty dancing elephants! (Not surprisingly, a rather strange conversation ensued when Stravinsky was called and asked to write this piece, "For what?" asked Stravinsky. "For elephants." "How many?" "A lot." "How old?" "Young." "If they're young, I accept.") If you want to hear something from his later, rather harsher pieces, I'd recommend particularly his last major work, 'Requiem Canticles' (which was played at his own funeral); it is strange, unearthly – and sombrely beautiful. If you want to hear something *really* weird, try his very last work, a song called 'The Owl and the Pussycat'; it's perfect music for children – for the children of extra-terrestials, that is! But of course, it's got something.

These are just a handful of the many and hugely varied works, of course; I'm pretty sure that you'll like some much more than others. Basically, I'd recommend that you start with those three ballets, especially 'The Rite' – and then go exploring...

Facts of Life

◄ ❶ ►

Stravinsky was born in St. Petersburg, Russia, in 1882. He had two older brothers whom he didn't really like, a father who was a famous singer but a very distant father, and a mother whom Stravinsky couldn't stand – he found her cruel and terrifying, even when she grew old. The only member of the family he really liked was his younger brother, Guri.

Early memories...

Stravinsky's first musical memories date from the Russian countryside, where his family used to spend the summers. He saw there was an enormous peasant with bright red hair, who couldn't talk, but could cluck two syllables in quick succession to make a song (of sorts). He'd accompany himself by making very rude noises with his hand squelching under his armpit. What an inspiration that must have been!
Stravinsky also developed his first taste for making money in the country. He and his brother Guri would capture spiders (probably harmless daddy-long-leg types), put them in jars, tell their friends that they were in fact deadly tarantulas, and charge a fee for viewing the dangerous beasts. "Profits were excellent," Stravinsky remembered proudly. Hmm...

◄ ❷ ►

Although he was always fascinated by music, Stravinsky was no prodigy; he didn't show any special talent as a youngster, and was forced by his parents to go to university and study law (like Schumann). The turning point came in 1902 when, at the age of twenty, Stravinsky was introduced to the famous composer Rimsky-Korsakov (wonderful name!). Rimsky encouraged him to study composition, but not at the St. Petersburg Conservatoire; he saw that Stravinsky was too original for such a conventional place. Stravinsky was first sent to a student of Rimsky's for lessons, and then went to the great man himself.

A second father...

Stravinsky loved Rimsky-Korsakov, who became like a second father to him – especially since Stravinsky's own father had died in 1902. Rimsky's death in 1908 devastated Stravinsky; but in later years, Stravinsky quarrelled with the Rimsky-Korsakov family, and ended up on very bad terms with them. When Stravinsky went back to Russia in 1962, Rimsky's daughter was invited to visit him, but she refused, "We didn't like each other fifty years ago, so why should we like each other now?" was her attitude.

Stravinsky married Catherine in 1906. Their wedding had to be a quiet one, held outside St. Petersburg with an unfussy priest, since the Russian Orthodox Church forbade first cousins to marry (each other, that is!). The couple were to have four children: Theodore, Ludmilla, Soulima and Milene.

A difficult family...

Stravinsky may not have been a great father. After all, it can't have been very nice for the children when he took up with Vera while their mother was still alive; and it must have been difficult for them to be quiet enough while their father was composing – but he did at least write fun pieces for them when they were young, and later made an effort to help them in their careers when they grew up. Soulima, a pianist, performed in many concerts with his father; and Stravinsky tried hard to get

*Theodore, an artist, work as a set designer in the theatre. But
sadly, Stravinsky and particularly Vera ended up on dreadful
terms with the surviving children at the end of Stravinsky's life.
There were legal battles and, at Stravinsky's funeral, the 'children'
(now in their fifties and sixties) and Vera totally ignored each
other – rather like a family in a television soap opera, but with a
sad ending.*

As a composer, Stravinsky shot to fame when 'The Firebird' was
performed by the 'Ballets Russes' (Russian Ballet) in Paris in
1910. The 'Ballets Russes' was a company masterminded by an
extraordinary character called Serge Diaghilev (Sergay Diaggilev
– sorry about all these Russian names!) His company created a
sensation with their seasons of operas and ballets in Paris and
other cities; nothing quite like it had ever been seen before!
Diaghilev had a genius for finding just the right dancers, singers,
choreographers (i.e. people who arranged the dances),
composers, painters (for scenery – always an important part of
his shows), costume-designers, writers etc. for his productions.
Almost overnight, thanks to Diaghilev, Stravinsky became a
famous man.

Wild times...

*It must have been really exciting for Stravinsky to be part of the
'Ballets Russes'. He met, and became friends with, many of the
greatest figures in the arts. They all took their work incredibly
seriously, convinced that they were changing the world; the
downside was that each one thought that his or her contribution
was the most important – i.e. the dancers and singers thought
that they were the stars; the choreographers thought that they had
created the show, which was just accompanied by the music in the
background; the writers thought their stories mattered most; and
the artists thought that their paintings and designs were the chief
attraction. You can imagine what Stravinsky thought was most*

important! So lots of quarrels ensued; but so did lots of fun. Sometimes there would be drunken parties, and Stravinsky might start jumping through hoops, or throwing cushions at all the other guests (if he were drunk enough). And sometimes it was extremely useful to be a celebrity: once, in Naples, Italy, Stravinsky and Pablo Picasso, probably the most famous painter of the twentieth century, had drunk too much and had to relieve themselves (or to put it more crudely – to pee!) against a wall. A policeman came across them in the act, and arrested them. They insisted that he take them to the local opera house – so he did, marching them along and keeping a thoroughly suspicious eye on the two louts. When they got to the opera house, though, and he saw everybody bowing and scraping to the two 'louts', the policeman vanished before you could say 'Stravinsky'. There was another time, too, that Stravinsky got into trouble because of Picasso. He was carrying a portrait of himself that Picasso had drawn in his unique modern style; some customs officers found it, looked at this extraordinary collection of shapes and squiggles, and confiscated it. They refused to believe that it was a portrait – they were sure that it was a coded war-plan!

Stravinsky became more and more famous, with 'Petrushka' being given its first performance in Paris by the Diaghilev company in 1911, and 'The Rite of Spring' riot taking place in 1913. But life wasn't all rosy: a few days after the riot, Stravinsky fell ill with typhoid fever, a dangerous illness. He recovered, but the next year World War One started and Stravinsky found himself in exile in Switzerland, cut off from his native Russia; he would not return to his homeland until 1962. Worse still, in 1917, the Russian Revolution broke out and Stravinsky found himself cut off from all his Russian *money!* He also quarrelled with Diaghilev, who travelled around with his company performing Stravinsky's works without paying him anything. Eventually, several of Stravinsky's admirers clubbed together and sent him a large sum. But, with his huge extended family to feed, these were troubled years.

A lost homeland – and lost income...

When the Russian Revolution destroyed the Russia Stravinsky had always known, there were various unpleasant consequences for him: for a start, his family and friends left in Russia were all in great danger. (His far-from-beloved mother survived, and a few years later came to live with Stravinsky – enough to put him in a permanent bad mood.) Then, even if he wouldn't have admitted it, he must have missed Russia, that land of magical snow, of passionate souls, of the folk traditions that so fascinated him. Also, the income from his compositions dried up, not only because Russian organisations couldn't pay him any more, but also because the works that were published in Russia – including 'The Firebird' – were no longer protected by international copyright laws, because the new Russian government wouldn't sign up to them. What this meant was that some of Stravinsky's works could be played anywhere in the world, without him being paid a penny; I'm sure he was thrilled! He made new revised versions, which he copyrighted; but he'd still lost a lot of money. His property in Russia was seized by the government, as well; and he also lost another, rather dubious source of income – he'd been lending money to his Russian relatives and demanding high interest on the loans. A funny combination – composer and money-lender. On the day he finished writing that astonishing

masterpiece, 'The Rite of Spring', he found that, having completed it in the morning, he had a free afternoon – so did he spend it pouring out grateful thanks for having completed this amazing landmark in musical history? No – he spent it writing letters demanding interest payments from his relatives! Not an inspiring story.

Stravinsky realised that he could make money much more quickly by performing than by composing. He'd always been very suspicious of performers anyway, and had spent a lot of time transcribing some of his pieces for mechanical piano, to cut out performers altogether; but when it became obvious that nobody was very interested in the mechanical piano, Stravinsky decided that he'd devote much more of his time to giving concerts himself. So, as the world returned to peace, he stepped up his concert tours, playing his own piano music and conducting his orchestral works around the world. Touring so much meant that he had less time for composing, but he still managed to produce quite a few masterpieces. He never really stopped composing, anyway; musical ideas were always occurring to him – once he had an idea on a plane, and had to write it down on toilet paper!

Conductors...

As a performer, Stravinsky was quite business-like (apart from the wonderfully deep, theatrical bow with which he used to greet his audiences); his concern was to get things right, not to give an emotional display. In fact, he kept a whole collection of photos of

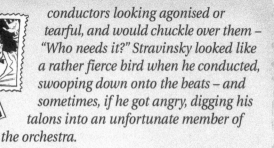

conductors looking agonised or tearful, and would chuckle over them – "Who needs it?" Stravinsky looked like a rather fierce bird when he conducted, swooping down onto the beats – and sometimes, if he got angry, digging his talons into an unfortunate member of the orchestra.

The late 1930s were a terrible time for Stravinsky. In late 1938, his eldest daughter, Ludmilla, died of tuberculosis (TB); three months later, Catherine followed her, dying of the same disease. Soon after that, World War Two broke out – but by then Stravinsky was safely in America. Vera followed him there, and they were married in 1940. They settled in the USA for the rest of their lives.

First things first...

*I'm sure that this was the worst time of Stravinsky's life; but it's difficult to know just how he felt. His music certainly gives no sign of his inner grief, but it **must** have been music – and Vera – that kept him going. Anyway, he didn't become any less selfish. A few years after he'd arrived in the USA, the situation there looked dicey, and Stravinsky asked a friend, very seriously, whether there might be a revolution. It was possible, the friend replied. Stravinsky was furious, "Where am I going to work, then?" he demanded indignantly. First things first...*

In 1948, Stravinsky received a letter from a young musician called Robert Craft, who was going to perform one of Stravinsky's lesser-known works in New York. Stravinsky took to the young man even before they'd met, actually offering to conduct part of the New York concert himself for free! Robert

(or Bob) Craft grew very close to the Stravinskys, and ended up living with them for the last twenty years of Stravinsky's life – becoming, perhaps, like the child that Stravinsky and Vera had never had together. For Stravinsky, Bob was a godsend: not only someone to help him with his everyday life, but also someone as intelligent (and frequently as angry, too) as himself. Craft introduced Stravinsky to music that he hadn't known at all, including lots of new music (to which Stravinsky had been so resistant in earlier years) – which is partly why Stravinsky's style suddenly changed, and became so much more modern. Practically, Craft was a huge help: he dealt with Stravinsky's correspondence, and even gave advice on Stravinsky's new compositions as they were written, trying them through with Stravinsky on the piano. (Not an entirely relaxing experience: Stravinsky would frequently stop to try out a chord, and then move on again without warning – and then he'd yell at Craft for not playing together with him!) Together, Stravinsky, Vera and Craft travelled round the world on concert tours – Craft rehearsing the orchestras that Stravinsky was going to conduct (often with Stravinsky sitting behind him in the hall, listening and conducting along – more relaxation therapy for Craft!) and in later years conducting half of Stravinsky's concerts for him, so that the older man could save his energy. (That can't have been easy for Craft, either: he was all too conscious, I'm sure, that some of the audience were only there to get a glimpse of the great composer. And he certainly wasn't given half the fee!) Stravinsky and Craft produced lots of books together, in the form of conversations between them; actually, they became increasingly Craft's books, but based on Stravinsky's opinions about music. There were reports in Stravinsky's last years of him lying on his bed, a helpless invalid, while Craft was writing articles in the next room and signing them 'Igor Stravinsky' – a strange thought. But then again, nobody (except Vera, perhaps) knew Stravinsky in his old age better than Craft did; and the books make very interesting reading for music-lovers.

The warmth of a son...

Craft's story is an unusual one. He basically gave up his youth for the Stravinskys: twenty-four years old when he met them, he was forty-seven when Stravinsky died. Meanwhile, he'd had to devote himself heart and soul to Stravinsky. I wonder what Stravinsky would have said if Craft had announced that he was moving out and getting married? He'd probably have been absolutely furious; anyway, it didn't happen. Also, many people from the Stravinskys' circle resented Craft's position in the household – none more than Stravinsky's children, of course. But for Craft, the excitement of life with the Stravinskys outweighed the difficulties; and he grew increasingly fond of the elderly couple. In his last years, Stravinsky came to rely more and more on 'Bob'; his chief pleasure was listening to music with him, following the printed score. By this time, it wasn't new music, or even Stravinsky's own works, that he wanted to hear; it was the music of the great composers of the past, especially Beethoven. After Stravinsky's death, Craft looked after Vera, again like the son she'd never had, until her death in 1982. As I write, Robert Craft is now married, has a son of his own, and is still very active as a conductor. In fact, he's recording a series of discs devoted to the music of – guess who? – Stravinsky!

Of all Stravinsky's concert tours, probably the most memorable was his return to Russia in 1962 – his first trip there for forty-eight years! Having declared during all the years of his exile that he didn't feel particularly Russian, Stravinsky changed his tune as soon as he got there. "A man has one birthplace, one fatherland, one country – he can only have one country – and the place of his birth is the most important factor in his life," he declared; quite a change of heart, especially for someone not exactly known for his emotional speeches. It wasn't a long trip, but it made a profound impression on Stravinsky – he didn't even talk about money while he was there!

While in Russia...

...Stravinsky went to a family reunion dinner in St. Petersburg given by his niece, who still lived in the apartment next to the one in which Stravinsky had grown up. She showed him a picture of his great-grandfather, Ignatievitch, who had lived until the age of 111 – and then died only because his family had ordered him not to go out at night, and locked the gate to his house; Ignatievitch tried to climb over the fence instead, and fell. On his eighty-fifth birthday, Stravinsky was asked if he'd like to follow Ignatievitch's example and live to 111, "No – taxes are too high now!" was the answer.

Eventually, Stravinsky grew too weak to conduct, and he had to give up; he would still charge fees, though, just to attend performances of his own works. (Even though his late works never became very popular with the public, his personal fame never diminished; even the Pope asked for his autograph!) In the end, sadly, he became too ill even to go to concerts. For the last couple of years of his life, he lived as an invalid in New York; these were difficult times – he wasn't an easy man to look after, by any means! His best days were those when he felt strong enough to listen to music, play the piano, even compose a little. He died in 1971 and, after funeral services in New York, his body was flown to Venice, the city of canals; here he was buried, amidst much pomp and ceremony – as well as lots of television cameras, getting in everyone's way – in a Russian Orthodox cemetery, near to the grave of his old friend, foe and champion Diaghilev. Vera is now buried next to her beloved husband.

Tough but tasty...

His last illness shrank Stravinsky; his voice sank to a whisper, his whisky had to be watered down to a mere taste, and he was frequently bedridden and apparently indifferent to his surroundings. But sometimes there were distinct flashes of the old Stravinsky, particularly in his attitude to his poor nurses. He'd throw a cushion at one of them or suddenly, seemingly from nowhere, summon the strength to bellow at them and give them a fright. Once, he complained to Vera, who had just engaged a new nurse for him, "I already have pains all over – why must you give me a pain in the neck, too?" Vera and Craft would know that he was having a good day if he looked around at the nurses and medical equipment and inquired anxiously, "How much is it costing?" Ah, Stravinsky... But there were touching moments, too: a few days before he died, Vera wanted him to sign his name on a letter. He took the pen, made sure she was watching, and, instead of his signature, wrote slowly: 'Oh, how I love you!' So all in all, there were many sides to Stravinsky. As he once said of himself, "If a lion eats me, you will hear the news from him. He will say that the old man was a tough, but tasty meal." Fair enough.

Chamber music

Pieces for two or more instruments with one player for each part. (Sonatas for two instruments count as chamber music.)

Chords

Groups of notes played at the same time.

Concerto

A piece, usually in three or four movements, for orchestra with one or more solo instrument(s). The solo instrument has more to do than the orchestral instruments, and usually gets to show off!

Conductor

The man or woman who stands in front of the orchestra, beating time and somehow managing to convey to the orchestra how the piece should sound. It's funny, that: the conductor doesn't actually make any noise, but an orchestra will sound quite different with one conductor than with another – magic!

Flute, clarinet, oboe, bassoon

'Woodwind' instruments: instruments that are blown, and are – or used to be – made of wood. (The materials have changed a bit in recent times; for instance, modern flutes are usually made of metal). All these instruments have distinctly separate personalities.

Harp, guitar

String instruments played without a bow, by plucking the strings; pop musicians play guitars, angels play harps.

Horn, trumpet, trombone, tuba, saxophone

'Brass' instruments: blown instruments that are made of – guess what? – brass; these can make a very loud noise!

Keys

As well as being the name for the things you press down on a piano to make sounds, the word 'key' has a larger meaning (in music, that is; nothing to do with locks and doors). Musical notes go from A up to G, and then start again on A; there are also some notes in between the seven main ones, which are known as 'sharp' or 'flat' notes. Each note has its own 'scale' (nothing to do with fish or weighing) – a series of notes beginning and ending on that note. There are two basic sorts of scales, the 'major' and the 'minor' which use different combinations of notes; the major tends to sound cheerful, the minor sad. Between the early seventeenth and early twentieth centuries, almost every piece had one of these scales as its 'home', with the main note known as the 'key' of the work. Each movement of the piece would start with notes taken from the home scale, go on a journey though lots of 'keys', and then come back to end on notes from the same scale. Phew! Complicated for a three-letter word, but a key is a good way of identifying a piece. For instance, if we talk about Brahms' G major violin sonata, people will instantly know which of his three violin sonatas we're talking about. Far more important, though, is the satisfying feeling one gets (even if one doesn't know why it is) from coming 'home' at the end of a long musical trip – as if the story has reached a proper ending.

Lieder

German for 'songs', generally for voice accompanied by piano.

Movement

A large section with its own beginning, middle and ending, complete in itself, but part of an even larger work; usually there are breaks between each movement of a piece – as there are between 'acts' in plays.

Opera

A play set to music, involving singers who also have to act, accompanied by an orchestra. Often features people dying tragically, but somehow managing to sing very loudly, and for quite a long time, as they expire.

Opus

Often shortened to 'op.': Italian for 'work'. Most composers' music is catalogued in order of 'opus'. For instance, the first works that Beethoven had published in Vienna are his three piano trios, op. 1, written when he was in his mid-twenties; the last works he wrote are his string quartets, op. 130-135.

Orchestra

A large group of musicians – playing wind instruments, string instruments, percussion instruments and (sometimes) keyboard instruments – who all make music together; an impressive sight and sound.

Percussion instruments

There are too many of these to list – but basically these are instruments that are hit with a stick (like drums or triangles), bashed together (like cymbals) or mistreated in some other way; and quite a racket they make about it, too.

Piano, harpsichord, organ

*Keyboard instruments, which can play more notes at the same time than other instruments; that's probably why virtually every composer's main instrument has been one of these. These instruments need dental help, though; they've all got lots of black teeth mixed up with the white ones. (All right, they're called 'keys' – goodness knows why – but they **look** like huge teeth.)*

Posthumous

*Often shortened to 'post.', means 'after death'. Many composers' last works are described as 'op. post.' This doesn't usually mean that they've written them after they've died, which would be tricky – just that the works have been **published** after they die.*

Quartets

Music for four players; string quartets are almost always written for two violins, viola and cello.

Quintets

Pieces for five instruments.

Sextets

Not what you think – just music for six instruments.

Sonata

A piece, often made up of three or four movements – usually written for one or two instruments.

Symphony

A piece – again, usually in three or four movements, for orchestra, with singers added occasionally.

Trios

Pieces for three players; most piano trios are for violin, cello and piano.

Violin, viola, cello, double-bass

'String' instruments – i.e. wooden instruments with four strings (made of either steel, or gut – from animals' insides!) played with a bow strung with horse-hair. Violins make the highest sound, violas are in the middle, cellos make a (lovely!) deep sound, and double-basses, lowest of all, are the grand-daddies.